THE PHOENIX AND THE FLAMES

THE PHOENIX AND THE FLAMES

BRENDAN LANDRY

ACKNOWLEDGEMENTS

It feels unreal that I'm writing this part of the book right now, but I wouldn't be writing it if it weren't for those who helped me along the way.

I would like to thank my family for everything they did throughout the entire process. Mom, Dad, Chris, Dylan, Kaitlyn, and Allie: I love you all. Thank you for the snaps, calls, texts, random sushi dates, and those times we came together and enjoyed each other's company. It may not seem like much, but every little thing you guys have done has kept the fire in my heart going strong. Thank you Mom and Dad for teaching me the values of patience and persistence. If it weren't for you guys, I would have given up on this dream a long time ago.

A huge thank you to Chris Moloney, Corinne Ferguson, Cameron Castillo, Danielle Garabo, and Zack Moore for being there for me through my ups and downs, and giving me the strength to stay motivated through the end. There were times I thought you guys were more excited about the book than I was, and I can't tell you how much that really kept me going.

Thank you to my editor, Michael Waitz, for the fine polishing and tuning.

Thank you Mark 'Mapo' Moran, and Mike 'Callie' Callahan for all the support and guidance. Next round is on me, fellas.

Last, but not least, I would also like to thank all those who showed me love, support, and guidance along the way. Whether I knew you or not, every little bit of encouragement or insight was appreciated. To name a few: Jennifer Sassano, Maria Schiaffo, Kristen Lange, Kevin Bottini, James Higgins, Tommy Gavin, Brett Bernard, Leonard Gjeloshi, Christina Hart, Alexxa Vanderbeek, and Samantha Kiernan.

Contents

CHAPTER 1: A LIGHT IN THE DARK

The void was deep and dark; black as the night. A shuffle of feet, and the scraping of a cloth bag on a rough stone floor reverberated off empty walls. The pattering of a steady rain paired with the occasional thunder penetrated the enclosed space. A man muttered to himself, fidgeting through the contents of the bag. The fidgeting soon stopped, but the inaudible muttering continued.

The rough sound of metal scraping upon flint created the first signs of light. Sparks followed each rhythmic flick until one found a home in the kindling on the ground. The tiny ember waned as it levitated from its spot, but grew larger with every whoosh of the man's breath. It caught the kindling and erupted into a small, but life-giving flame. It fell back down to the ground where the twigs piled on top of it lost their battle to smother its existence. And now the tiny little ember, contagious in its actions, created a light for the world to see.

"Let there be light," spoke the man in a raspy voice.

His faint outline flickered in the glow of the fire, but his features and surroundings became clearer with every passing second. His wavy, unkempt hair fell over a set of broad shoulders. The animal-skin coat draped over his back cast a fearsome shadow against the tall stone walls of the enclosure. Large stone slabs surrounded the well-used campfire, acting as makeshift seats.

The man reached into his sack once more and pulled out a freshly killed rabbit. He skinned the rabbit with ease before mounting it on a stick.

"I'm going to eat well tonight," he chuckled as he rested the meat above the fire.

Without warning, the door behind him burst open. The man pulled a pistol from inside his coat and directed his attention towards the door. A figure stood in the doorway, his silhouette outlined by a perfectly timed bolt of lightning. "Don't move, or this will be the last thing you see," said the man by the fire.

"Relax, Robbie!" the other figure replied. "You wouldn't shoot an old friend, would ya?"

Robert recognized the owner of that voice.

"Depends on how many times they've tried to kill me."

Robert returned his pistol to his coat and turned back towards the fire.

"What about over old bets?" the figure replied again. "A pack of smokes and 3 beers is what you owe if I remember correctly."

Robert grinned, remembering the game of chess he'd lost those years ago.

"A debt I can settle right now. Now get in here and close that damn door. It's coming down heavy out there."

The man pressed the door hard against the wind before finally managing to close it. He pulled the fedora off his head, shaking off the excess rain before walking over and taking a seat next to Robert.

He was a tall man in his mid-forties, with a gray streak running through his combed brown hair. His clean-shaven face held a set of light brown eyes which Robert could now see in the dancing light of the fire.

"So this is what you've been doing this whole time," the new figure said, looking around the inside of the tower.

"Living the quiet life, yes," replied Robert.

He pulled a corked glass bottle from his sack. The satisfactory pop of the cork echoed through the chamber as he tipped the bottom of the bottle towards the ceiling. The amber liquid inside raced towards the neck and into Robert's mouth. He lowered the bottle and let out a hearty sigh of satisfaction before handing the drink to his guest. Robert then pulled two cigarettes from his pocket and lit them both in the crackling fire.

"I'm going to skip the pleasantries and cut to the chase," said Robert, clearing his throat. "Why are you here, Joe?"

Joe took a drink and winced as the fiery liquid slid down his throat. He then grabbed the second lit cigarette from Robert, taking a quick drag before continuing.

"Why else?" he coughed. "Government business would be the only thing urgent enough to come out here during the winter."

Robert took another drag of his cigarette and looked Joe in the eye.

"If you expect you can just walk in here and convince me to stand trial, you're wrong. Should have sent a Ghost team instead."

Joe took a swig and passed the bottle back to Robert.

"Who said anything about standing trial? No, we want to pull you out of retirement."

"So go back to doing the government's dirty work? Is that what you're asking me to do?"

"I'm not asking you to do anything," defended Joe. "I'm just relaying the message. But I suggest you think about it. Face it, you can't run forever. Every time we catch up to you, you escape by the skin of your teeth. Top brass will never call off the hunt, and it's only a matter of time before your luck runs out. They want you sentenced for treason, and for your unauthorized leave from the HIVE."

"The first and only one to break out!" interrupted Robert. "Gotta count for something, right?"

Joe laughed.

"You know that won't help."

He glanced into his lap before turning his attention back at Robert.

"But Marcella would, and *has*. She's kept her knowledge of your whereabouts a secret, and is willing to grant you your freedom if you cooperate."

"So she knew where I was this whole time."

"Well, no. Your trail went cold for quite some time, but a few months ago one of our drones caught you sleeping in a field in the Western Penns. It tagged you, and you led us here."

Joe took another drag of his cigarette, looking at it with disgust before condemning it to the heart of the fire.

"What I don't get," he continued, "is why you came back here. Of all the places you could go, you still decided to come here."

Robert laughed as he looked into the fire.

"The summers are lazy, the fall is gorgeous, and there aren't many people or patrols out here. Especially during the rainy months. Besides, I do like to return home every now and then. Was hoping to see some beautiful fall colors before I left again, but it looks like that's not going to happen."

Joe grinned.

"Hiding under our noses was pretty smart. After losing track of you in the West a few years ago, the last place we would have expected to find you was here."

He then shifted himself into a more comfortable position before continuing.

5

"This is your chance to end this once and for all. You don't have to go on the run again. Do these few jobs for her, and you'll be free to live any life you want."

Robert leaned away from Joe and studied him for a moment.

"And what if I refuse?" he asked. "I could kill you right now and disappear again."

"You could, but if I come back with bad news; or don't report back at all, the entire New Amsterdam military will be scouting these woods by daybreak. Once the word reaches the other city states, they too will send their forces."

"They're not holding any punches, are they?"

"Like I said, top brass has wanted you for a long time. They don't intend to take any chances with arguably the most dangerous man on the continent. But don't get me wrong, they will look to take you alive. That means you will stand trial and be sent to Eisenstadt. And we all know—"

"It's a fate worse than death," finished Robert.

Robert took a quick drag of his cigarette and weighed his options. Refusal would mean potentially ending up in Eisenstadt, not to mention an end to his quiet life. Accepting the deal meant diving head first into the world he walked away from all those years ago. It would save him from Eisenstadt, but it still wouldn't guarantee his freedom. It was a decision Robert knew he couldn't make lightly.

"How would a disavowed enemy of the state enter the HIVE?" he asked.

"That's where I come in," Joe said with a grin.

He pulled a case from his pocket and opened it in front of Robert. Inside was a simple injector loaded with a tiny capsule.

"Marcella saw to it that facial and retinal scanners in New Amsterdam will no longer identify you as a high-priority target. She also gave me a rewritten tag. Level 1 and Zone 1 clearance, under the alias Captain Leonard Smeebly of the Joint HIVE Defense Force."

Robert grunted in disgust.

"You couldn't pick a better name?" he asked, "and since when do you guys use implanted tags?"

Joe laughed.

"Just be glad you got one. Otherwise you'd be breaking in the same way you got out."

He cleared his throat before continuing.

"The tags are just a slight precaution. Some lower zone inhabitants learned they could hide their faces from the retinal and facial scanners, and were regularly breaching Zone 2. With this bad boy, anyone who goes where they don't belong will get a warning shock. If they don't comply in one minute, the tag releases cyanide into their system. Any attempt to remove it will do the same."

Robert picked the injector out of its case and examined its sleek, metallic body.

"Hmmm. Simple, yet effective. I'm assuming this one has no cyanide?"

"You are correct," replied Joe. "Zone 1 clearance is the ultimate clearance. You can go anywhere."

Robert pushed the injector into his arm and depressed the plunger. The injector punched the capsule into his flesh, leaving a telltale hexagonal imprint on the skin.

"So you're in?" asked Joe.

"Not exactly," replied Robert as he handed back the injector. "I need to get in and discuss my terms with Marcella. If that goes well, I'm in."

Robert rotated the stick holding the rabbit over the fire, and took another swig from the bottle.

"You're welcome to stay for food if you want. We'll need our strength to make our way back to the HIVE."

Joe shook his head.

"I'm not returning with you. Have some business to attend to at another HIVE. But I will stay for some food. It has been a while since I've eaten something good."

"Don't tell me the food in there is horrible," Robert said. "I'm too old to be living off military rations again."

Joe shrugged.

"It's all fresh, but something just always seems...off. Like the plants know they've gone their whole life without ever feeling the warmth of a real sun."

Robert listened, but was firm with his previous judgment.

"As long as there's more instructions than 'Just add water' I'll be fine."

Robert held the bottle out towards Joe.

"More whiskey?"

Joe looked at it with reluctance, but grabbed it anyway. He took a swig and winced as the alcohol once again singed the inside of his throat.

"How did you get your hands on alcohol and cigarettes out here?" He coughed.

Robert smirked as he took another drag from his cigarette.

"The alcohol was easy. Spent the whole summer making it a few years back."

Joe handed back the bottle and Robert took a long, hearty swig before continuing.

"And as for the cigarettes, I stumbled upon these by chance. Found a whole shipment in one of those end-of-the-world bunkers nearby. Guy musta thought cigarettes would be good currency."

Joe shook his head and smiled.

"If only they'd known what the world would be now."

"Well if they had, then I would be down a lifetime supply of cigarettes, wouldn't I?"

They laughed as Robert took the rabbit off of the fire and laid it on a large wooden plate beside him.

"At least you only saw the aftermath, Joe," added Robert. "Some had to watch the whole thing."

They divided up the rabbit and ate in silence, savoring every bit as if they would never eat again. After dinner, Robert prepared a comfortable place for Joe to rest, and lay down himself before drifting into his last slumber as a free man.

CHAPTER 2: WALKING OLD PATHS

Robert woke up the next day to the long-awaited absence of rain pattering on the roof. He hobbled his way over to the door and pushed it open to let the blinding radiance of the morning sun pierce the inside of the tower. Though his eyes still needed time to adjust, Robert smiled at the orange glow which penetrated his eyelids. Despite the chill of the winter wet season hanging in the surrounding air, the light warmed Robert's face like the hot fire inside the tower. He stood there for a moment to appreciate the sun's return from its vacation behind the clouds. Once his eyes grew accustomed to the light, Robert walked out of the tower towards the edge of the old overgrown parking lot before him.

He looked out and laid his eyes on the perfect view from atop the mountain. A thick fog blanketed the valley below, sparing only the tops of the surrounding ridges from

11

its embrace. It was a beautiful sight. The first signs of the spring revival poked out between the clusters of evergreens and bare rock outcrops on the adjacent peaks. Even a couple feet in front of him, Robert could see the trees and shrubs awakening from their slumber.

Despite the serenity of the natural beauty surrounding him, Robert could still make out the faint outline of the concrete jungle standing guard at the distant mouth of the Hudson River. He gazed at it as its gloomy outline faded in and out of the fog.

"I really have to go back," he thought in disbelief.

He wished the memory of the night before were just a bad dream. But the note he found lying next to him when he awoke reinforced the reality of the situation.

Be at Phoenix Tower by noon tomorrow. Don't be late. You know what is at stake.

Joe.

Robert knew exactly what was at stake. He once again thought about running. Hell, he knew those woods better than anyone alive. The prospect of running for the rest of his life, or even worse, being caught, was more than enough to deter him from turning back now. He knew striking a deal with Marcella was his only chance of living in real peace.

"I guess I'd better get moving," he sighed to himself. *"Got some things to pick up anyways."*

Robert took one last look at the surrounding valley before journeying down the driveway to the bottom of the mountain. Following the lonesome road sank him deeper and deeper into the mist-filled valley, and soon he couldn't see but a couple yards in front of him. The dense moss blanketing the ground cushioned each step, and the red maple blossoms decorating the understory caused the fog above him to shine a magnificent red. Scant bird calls and rustling leaves broke the silence, causing Robert to grin at spring's long-awaited arrival.

The fog thinned as Robert reached the end of the driveway and found the path carved down the middle of the main road. Although bushes and grass covered most of the asphalt, the faint markings of painted lines showing through the center of the trail reminded him of a time when these stretches of pavement were in use.

"Oh, if only I could go back for one day," he said to himself.

He reminisced about riding his motorcycle through these mountain roads all those years ago. The roar of the engine between his legs. The whirring of the tires as he carved through the twists and turns. The way her hands held him tightly from behind. But at that final memory he shook the thought out of his mind and brought himself back to the overgrown state of the present.

"If only I could."

This place brought back so many memories, yet no matter how far he traveled, or how long he was gone, Robert always found himself returning to the forested lands he once called home. They were the only thing left from his life before the war. The only reminder of a simpler and happier time.

Robert followed the trail deeper into the valley until the dense forest opened to a vast, grassy field dotted with clusters of shrubs and young Juniper trees. The fog hugging the landscape subsided, allowing the sun to cast its golden rays upon the tender green shoots poking up amidst the dead stalks from last season.

Robert wished he could clear a spot in the field and lie down to celebrate the advent of spring, but he knew it wasn't an option. So off he went, venturing deeper down the trail as it meandered through the grass and brush. After a few minutes, his destination came into view.

At the edge of the field, nestled at the foot of the mountain he just descended, stood the remains of his father's estate. Rounded granite fieldstones held together with mortar made up the first floor and the staircase leading to the wooden structure above. Lichens and moss encrusted the stone, creating the illusion that the building merely sprouted from the ground. Some trees behind the building separated it from a quiet lake shimmering in the morning sun.

"Home, sweet home," Robert said as he continued towards the estate.

Robert passed through the rusty remains of the fence surrounding the building and ascended the staircase to the front door. It was cast-iron and had a basin protruding from the door at about waist height. Inscribed a foot above it were a few words.

"Those of true courage may open this door. Those who know true order may find the door already open."

Robert remembered his frustration when he found the old wooden door replaced by the new metal one. He sat outside for days wondering what the riddle meant, and why his father didn't give him the key. But then again, everything was a riddle when it came to his father.

"And if there's one thing I know about true order," he said to himself as he turned around and climbed onto the staircase's stone railing, "it's that it doesn't exist."

Robert then grabbed the ledge above him and hoisted himself onto the shale roof. He walked to the edge of the roof on the left side of the building and jumped down onto a small third-story balcony overlooking the lake. The aged timber creaked underneath his forceful landing, but still held true. Robert brushed himself off and opened the fragile door leading inside. He stepped inside and found himself on a balcony overlooking a vast library. A double staircase descended from either side of him into the labyrinth of bookcases below. The only available light in the room came from a glass skylight. The sun's rays shone through the stale air, illuminating the row of book-filled tables running the length of the room.

Robert's vision adjusted as he made his way down the staircase, and he soon realized something wasn't right. "Someone's been here," he said as he looked upon the mess. Several bookcases lay empty, their contents strewn across the floor as if someone tore them from their resting place. Robert wanted to stop everything and track down the people who had desecrated his favorite room in the manor, but the dust collecting on the book jackets told him they were long gone. For now, all Robert had were the memories of the times he spent here as a child, and the long rainy months he weathered there when he hid from the HIVE. He remembered using the automated librarian to find all the books his father read, and to read them all. Robert smiled at the memory of the librarian always putting the books in the same spot on the table. He thought about starting up his old friend again, but knew the lack of power would keep him from working. Robert walked past the faded pages of the books left open on the table, but he froze as he approached the very end. A lone book sat in the very spot the librarian used to put the requested books. All the books around it were pushed away as if to make room. "Librarian, are you there?" called Robert, but the room remained silent. Robert approached the crimson, hard-covered book and wiped the dust from the gold letters on its face. "*The Gatekeeper's Key*, by Charles Sunterberry," he said aloud.

Robert picked up the book, noting its size and weight as it rested in his grasp. He wanted to know of the contents stored within the pages, but was well aware of what happened to pre-war books found within the veil of the HIVE. Anyone caught sneaking them inside would share the same fate — destruction. Robert thought about leaving the book, but decided to stash it in his bag and walk out the door leaving the library.

Entering this door led him into a long hallway lit by a single window at the end. The dust and cobwebs covering every surface were so thick that even the act of stepping on the floor created footprints. It reminded him of how long it'd been since he last stepped foot in these halls.

The times then were different. The solar panels on top of the house were functional. Though they captured a great deal of energy in the summer months, they were useless in the dark and rainy months of winter when they were needed for heating and running the greenhouse lights. To overcome this flaw, the batteries connected to the solar panels sent any extra energy to a pump. In turn, the pump moved water from the lake to a reservoir on the mountain. When the batteries ran low on energy, the reservoir released the water through a hydroelectric turbine to recharge the batteries. Since the system was designed for a world with power plants, the reservoir only held enough water to power the entire house for a month. Robert needed to make it last four.

Robert used the house to help brave the winters he spent in the area until one day the panels stopped working. He searched long and hard to fix the issue, only to find the panels themselves beyond repair. Without the ability to reliably grow food in the winter, Robert had very little reason to return.

Navigating the hallway led him towards an open foyer. The windows lining the wall to his right gave him a perfect view of the field in front of the manor, and the staircase leading up to the cast-iron door tucked into the corner of the room. To his left was another hallway which led deeper into the house, and in front of him was a long desk which ran along the wall. Behind the desk was a set of cubbies which straddled yet another cast iron door. Robert walked across the room, vaulted over the desk, and wrenched open the door to slip inside.

The small study waiting for him on the other side held a large desk with an equally large portrait hanging on the wall behind it, a full bookcase along the right wall, and a mirror along the left. The balding man in the portrait had a crooked nose, and thick gray eyebrows which matched his hair. His green eyes appeared to bore into Robert's soul, making him avert his gaze as he stepped towards the desk. The papers cluttering the desktop covered almost every square inch, but left just enough room for a black desk lamp and a metal name plaque at the corner of the desk. Despite the heavy layer of dust, Robert could still make out the name engraved on the plaque.

Sebastian Phoenix

He picked it up and wiped its metallic face.

"What happened to you, dad?"

Memories of his father flooded his head, almost bringing tears to Robert's eyes. He remembered all the nature walks with him, and all the lessons his father taught him. How they laughed together, and how they talked for hours on end whenever they had the chance to get together. But the day of his father's disappearance filled his head. How he vanished without a trace and was presumed dead. The wake. The funeral. How Robert couldn't accept his father's death, and the cryptic note his father left him.

Robert returned the plaque and focused his attention on the topmost piece of paper on the desk. The folded page lay open, exposing the faded ink scribbled onto the paper.

My Dearest Robert,

If you are reading this, then I am no longer with you. It also means that I'm leaving you a bunch of my belongings, including the Phoenix Manor and everything within it. I simply can't take it with me where I'm going, all I can carry are ideas. The manor and its belongings are yours to squander or treasure however you choose, but as my last request to you I beg for it to be kept safe. It is more valuable than you will ever know. Don't worry, my son, everything will make sense when the time is right.

Love Always,

Dad

P. S.—Whenever you feel weak, the mirror can show you strength you never knew existed.

Robert walked over to the mirror and gazed into its vast depths. He almost didn't recognize himself through his wild-like appearance, but the bright blue eyes staring back at him in the mirror assured him the reflection was true. Robert couldn't remember the last time he'd looked in a mirror, and once again his mind wandered towards the past. The last time he looked into this mirror was shortly after his leaving the HIVE. Shaven face. Short hair. A rage in his heart he couldn't tame. Robert felt the rage build up as his

19

old wounds tore open all over again, but Robert fought the rage and snapped himself back to reality.

"*Everything has two meanings,*" he thought.

This was something he learned from the many riddles and mysteries his father left him over the years. And just as he did upon first discovering the note, he looked past his own reflection towards the bookcase behind his right shoulder.

The bookcase held various genres of books, but the ones which stood out were volumes T, F, L, and E from an incomplete dictionary set. It originally took Robert a long time to figure this out, but the graining in the wood at the top of the bookcase also appeared to read 'LEFT' when looked at through the mirror. So Robert walked over to the shelf and arranged the dictionary volumes so they lined up with their corresponding letters on the wood. With that, the bookcase swung outward from the wall, revealing a staircase down to the first floor.

At the bottom of the staircase was a windowless room which opened up to his left. The tall glass ceiling allowed the sun's rays to illuminate every crack and crevice, making all of its contents easy to see. Racks, benches, and cases full of an array of weapons and gadgets lined the far wall. The center of the room held two large objects draped with blankets.

Robert walked over to the far wall and opened a wooden wardrobe. A dusty black coat with long tails hung next to an armor-plated vest. Below them was a folded pair of black pants resting upon a worn pair of black boots. Just the sight of his vest brought back memories of all the people he met and the places he went during his time of service. Whether he was fighting in a full-scale ground war, or conducting covert assassination missions, Robert never went on a mission without it. This time would be no different.

Robert took the knapsack off of his back and stripped off his old worn clothes, replacing them with the ones inside the cabinet. He finished dressing and laid his eyes on the final piece of his uniform. His combat gauntlets sat in their own separate case within the closet. They were fingerless, with a Kevlar plate stretching the length of his forearm.

Robert slipped them on and felt the familiar pinch of the gauntlets tapping into his nervous system. Robert tapped on the guard on his right arm and it sprang to life. The hidden screen amongst the Kevlar illuminated as the hardware loaded its programming. He moved his wrist around, and with just the power of his thoughts, a sharp, retractable dagger extended from the underside guard of the gauntlet

"Good, they still work," he said.

Robert wasn't sure the hardware of his father's creations would stand the test of time, but he always had faith in the power source. These gauntlets were among the few known remaining items powered by a Phoenix Core—a nearly unlimited power source created by Phoenix Technologies. The Phoenix Core was expected to become the power source of the future, but a cyber-attack only days after Sebastian's death erased all the blueprints and evidence of his father's work. Many attempts were made to reverse-engineer the core, but all failed. Robert wished his father had shared the secret, but sadly it was one of the many things lost to the war.

Robert loaded his backpack with an extra pistol, a knife, and a few boxes of ammo. The rifles hanging on the wall were tempting, but he didn't want to chance drawing attention as he tried to enter the HIVE. Two pistols would have to do for the time being.

Robert then walked over to one of the draped objects. He grabbed a crease on the cover and ripped it off to reveal an old motorcycle. The straight leather seat and the gleaming Gunmetal Grey paint made it look like it had just rolled off the factory floor. The words 'Hydrogen Rotary Engine' were emblazoned across the metal engine casing.

The memories of riding this motorcycle all those years ago came flying back again, but he stopped them before they could take hold.

"It's time to go," he thought.

With his sack over his shoulder, Robert mounted the bike. He turned on the ignition and kicked the engine to life in one swift motion. The little engine spat as if clearing out a decade's worth of cobwebs, but soon fell into a steady idle. Robert then opened a set of garage doors in front of him, letting in the natural light. When the bike was finally warmed up, he clicked it into gear and rode into the bright world outside.

CHAPTER 3: ENTERING THE HIVE

"So this is it," Robert thought.

He clicked the bike into neutral and flipped the visor on his helmet. The little engine between Robert's legs purred its calm idle as he looked across the long suspension bridge traversing the depths of the murky water below. The rusted cables strung along its two spans ended at what appeared to be a collection of stacked debris on the far end. A concrete wall lining the opposite shore stretched as far as the eye could see. Only the tallest buildings broke the wall's horizon, and even they were clouded by the pearlescent dome of energy capping the entire city.

Robert sat there for a while and stared across the span of water dividing him from the HIVE. This was the point of no return. This was his last chance to turn back.

He could easily turn the bike around and ride until he ran out of hydrogen, but he knew this was the only way.

This was his only chance to bargain a peaceful resolution with Marcella. Robert sighed one last breath before clicking the bike back into gear and beginning the journey across.

A slight breeze caused the bridge to creak and groan as Robert weaved between the husks of decaying cars. The pavement below his tires popped and crumbled under his weight, daring to give way at any moment. Unsettling thoughts of plunging into the river below flooded Robert's mind, but still he pushed forward.

As he made his way across the bridge, the heap of metal at the end of it took shape. The rough edges formed into the outlines of elaborate shacks made from the remains of the old world. Faint columns of smoke rose from the makeshift village, filling the air with the foul scent of wood and trash. Robert reached the edge of the shantytown and soon realized its full extent. The multi-storied shacks covered most of the bridge, leaving a path only a single lane of traffic wide. Hundreds of people lined the alley, all shouting and bartering for the goods from the market stands in front of the shacks.

Robert shut off his motorcycle and walked it into the crowd. He pushed his bike between the groups of people and tried his best to be inconspicuous. Some didn't even notice him, while others shot untrusting looks at the man they knew didn't belong. But Robert didn't mind the stares as long as they didn't notice him walking down the street with a rolling gold mine.

The crowd thinned as Robert once again reached the outskirts of the town. He almost reached the clearing between the town and the wall when he felt a tug on his coat.

"Wow mister, now that's a find!"

Robert turned around to find a young boy gleaming at his motorcycle. He tried to brush the kid off, but the little boy latched on tightly and turned to wave at a nearby crowd.

"Hey poppa, look what this man got!"

Robert's heart sank as all the nearby people fixed their eyes on his motorcycle.

"This isn't good," he thought.

Fending off would-be looters wasn't part of the plan, but neither was losing his motorcycle. Robert knew he needed to distract them, and he had something which just might work. He pulled a pouch of coins from his pocket, loosened the draw string, and tossed it into the space behind him. The sound of the change chiming against the ground acted as a dinner bell. Almost instantaneously the crowd closed in on his pouch, scraping up anything they could find. Robert seized the moment and pushed his motorcycle towards the safety of the clearing.

"That was a close call," he thought, *"but now comes the moment of truth."*

He made his way out of the shanties and continued towards the wall. Armed soldiers and a single armored tower guarded the large gate. In front of the tower was a large metal sign.

"SCRAP METAL FOR FOOD. TECHNOLOGY FOR CITIZENSHIP."

He continued to walk towards the gate, keeping his mind relaxed. As he approached, he realized there was a woman interacting with one of the guards. Robert saw her pull a toaster from her sack and present it to the guard, causing him to laugh in her face.

"Hah, you expect to pay for your passage with that? Try coming back with a couple hundred more and I'll think about it."

"But please sir!" the woman begged. "I need work to feed my children."

"Then take the one ration that it's worth and get lost!"

The woman got down on her knees and held up the toaster.

"I beg you, sir!"

"I said GET LOST!"

The guard swung his arm and backhanded the woman across the face, sending her tumbling to the ground. He then threw the ration at her while mumbling some smart remark under his breath. The woman sobbed as she picked up the ration and hobbled back towards the shantytown.

Unfazed, Robert rolled his bike up to the guard and rested it on the kickstand. The guard gleamed at the prize wheeled before him.

"Ah, now that's what I'm talking about."

He went to reach for the handlebars, but Robert stepped in front of him and slapped his hand out of the way.

"It's not for sale," he said.

The guard glared at Robert for the insulting blow to his hand, but Robert returned eye contact and kept calm.

"You better have a good reason for touching me," the guard stated through clenched teeth.

At that Robert pulled back his sleeve and exposed the scar where he'd injected the tag. The guard smirked as if he caught another beggar trying to lie their way into the city.

"Ahh so you got good blood now, do ya? I hope you know the punishment for lying to a Guardsman."

The guard scanned Robert's arm with delight, but his face soon turned to shock as his scanner's screen filled with information. After staring at the screen for a moment, the guard waved for Robert to pass.

"All right you're good to go. Now head into containment for twenty-four-hour screening."

This is what Robert hoped to not happen. The full screening would reveal his contraband and blow his cover. Luckily, Robert had come with one more trick up his sleeve.

"That will not be necessary. I have urgent business to attend to."

The guard looked at him with disgust.

"Then get the hell out of here! I don't care if you're the Governess herself. Everyone that's not from this HIVE goes through the screening."

"Well then I'll make sure to tell her how rudely she would be received at her own city."

Robert straightened himself up and tried to act as pompous as possible before continuing.

"I am Captain Smeebly of the Joint HIVE Defense Force. The Governess sent me to recover a very important object, and needs to see me right away."

He then slung the bag off of his shoulder and pulled out a transparent glass cube about the size of a softball. Suspended in the middle was a molten ball of fire and light. Robert had found it years ago in his father's study, but never knew what it was. It looked like a sun in a box, and probably was. But since his father left it lying around in his office, Robert assumed he used it to demonstrate the ability of Phoenix Technologies. Despite its original use, Robert usually used it as a flashlight.

Robert held it out and accidentally gave it a tight squeeze. The cube sprang to life and started to levitate from his hand as the soft white light emanating from the molten core grew into a bright yellow. The guard stared in amazement. Even Robert fought to hold back his disbelief.

"What the hell is this thing?" he thought.

Suddenly the cube tilted one of its points towards the ground and began to spin like a top. The inner core turned a hue of orange as it gained speed.

"Ok that's a little too far," he thought.

Robert reached out to grab it, and luckily another squeeze brought the cube back to its resting state.

The guard still stood there dumbfounded by the occurrence, but quickly dropped to his knee and bowed his head.

"My apologies, Captain. I did not recognize you in your current attire."

"Well, let this be a lesson for you to never judge someone by their appearance," replied Robert.

He placed the cube back into his bag and lifted his motorcycle off the kickstand before continuing.

"And be glad I am merciful. Others my rank would have you stripped down and sent to Eisenstadt."

He rolled his bike past the guard and made his way towards the opening gate.

"Maybe a bit overdramatic," he chuckled to himself, *"but it did the trick."*

The heart of the wall was dark, making it near impossible for Robert to see where he was walking. But as he broke the horizon into the darkness, the lights flickered on above him. The barriers in the road led him towards a small pedestrian tunnel. Robert followed it and found himself face to face with two more armed guards lining either side of a body scanner. As he got closer, the two guards came to attention and simultaneously raised their hands into a salute. Robert played along and saluted back with relative speed. A screeching alarm pierced the air as he passed through the scanner, but to Robert's surprise, the guards didn't react.

"So this is how it feels to be connected again. Just waltz right into the city."

The tunnel led into a cubic room with polished white walls that mirrored his reflection. Robert entered as the door behind him closed and an automated voice came over the loudspeaker.

"Dear Sir or Madam, I welcome you with open arms to the grand city of New Amsterdam! We are excited to have you here, and can assure you made the right choice. After all, New Amsterdam was the pioneer city in the Habitation In Volatile Environments; or, HIVE program. We continue to boast our city's position on the cutting edge of technological advancements, and are proud to provide them for our aspiring, and well-educated populace. Please allow us to take this time to clear you of all possible contaminants while also providing you with more information. Relax! The screening and cleaning are both non-invasive procedures, and are necessary to maintain the level of cleanliness we uphold in our fine city. Just sit tight and it will be over before you know it."

Tiles in the ceiling opened, allowing robotic arms to drop down and scan Robert with their beams. He watched as his jacket grew cleaner with each passing ray. He could even feel the dirt lifting from his hair and skin.

"While we proceed, let me inform you more about the city's rich history. The HIVE program was founded in 2029 by the late entrepreneur Sebastian Phoenix, who saw the need for a refuge from an increasingly hostile world. His vision was realized by Governor Raedbeck of New York, who granted Phoenix the rights to encompass New York City and its northern suburbs in his project. The success of New Amsterdam led to the completion of several more around the country on order of President Miller of the former United States."

Robert grunted with annoyance at the history lesson.

"Are you done yet?" he asked as he stuck a cigarette in his mouth.

But before he could light it, one of the arms snatched it from his mouth and retracted into the ceiling.

"Smoking is prohibited in the decontamination room, sir."

Robert was ready to reply with a distasteful comment, but the voice continued the audio tour without even skipping a beat.

"Global conflict erupted seven years later, and soon the world was on the brink of human extinction. After more than a decade of global destruction, the Freedom party took over and forged the lasting peace you see today. And from the remaining HIVEs they formed the Eastern American Union."

The arms stopped scanning and retracted into the ceiling, but the voice continued with its final remark.

"It appears everything is good to go! Thank you for your patience and cooperation. You may proceed through the doors ahead where you will receive your zone and living assignments. And remember to stay up to date on the latest Phoenix Technologies products!"

Robert shook his head and laughed to himself.

"The story was touching, but you may have skipped over a few important details."

The wall in front of Robert opened up, allowing Robert to walk down the passageway behind it. The hallway continued on a few hundred more feet before leading into a grand, open room. Pillars lined the walls, holding up the domed ceiling. The paintings and furnishings in the room showed its age, and the dust which layered the light granite floor showed its disuse. Robert pulled out a cigarette and double-checked for any retractable arms before lighting it up. He continued forward and rolled his bike down the long ramp to the main floor.

Robert remembered this place well. It was the first processing station of the HIVE. He walked past the empty mazes of stanchions, which once held hour-long queues of people waiting for registration. There was no longer the occasional rumble of subway trains taking newcomers to their zones emanating from the ground beneath his feet. It was like he entered a ghost town.

Robert crossed through another unused body scanner and strode towards the light coming through the high windows in front of him. At last he rounded one last vendor's stand, bringing the doorway into sight. There were a few doors, each with a personal scanner. Robert approached one of them and examined it. They were older models which could not read the tag in his arm.

"Well this is where we see if Joe was true to his word," he said to himself.

Robert placed his face in front of the glass tennis ball-sized dome. A light above the door turned yellow as the scanner searched its database. Moments later the door in front of him slid open, letting a blinding ray of light penetrate the room. The familiar automated voice came through the speaker attached to the scanner.

"Welcome back, Robert Phoenix."

CHAPTER 4: THE TWISTING OF FATES

"Why is everything so....bright?"

Robert looked into the brightness from the shadows of an old parking garage next to the processing station. Maybe it was because decades had passed since he last stepped foot in any city, but Robert stepped out of the processing station like a deer in headlights. Blinding light attacked him from all directions, and he had no choice except to navigate by staring down at the floor. He found the parking garage by chance, and thankfully he did. The darkness helping his eyes adjust also proved to be a useful place to hide his motorcycle for the time being.

The city streets were no longer painted with lines to mark the lanes or crossings. And now that he noticed, there wasn't any vehicle traffic on the street. One quick sweep of the parking garage confirmed Robert's suspicion.

"Well, I guess no one drives anymore."

The parking garage lay empty except for a handful of cars. They all sat on flat tires as they collected dust in their forgotten state. It seemed cars and motorcycles were a thing of the past, meaning Robert needed to leave his here to avoid suspicion. He found a good spot to park and waited for his eyes to adjust before heading towards his destination.

Jumping into the flow of pedestrian traffic immersed him in a feeling both foreign and familiar. Walking along the crowded sidewalk reminded Robert of New Amsterdam, but it wasn't the New Amsterdam he remembered. Everyone wore similar styles of neutral-colored clothing, the only difference being the color of the accents. There were no signs posted on the storefronts or corners; there weren't even traffic lights for cars and pedestrians. Yet the people surrounding him continued to walk within the confines of the sidewalks and crosswalks. To make things worse, the reflective sheen covering almost every square inch of hard surface made it hard for Robert to see without getting blinded or disoriented.

"How do people deal with this without puking?" thought Robert, *"and how do people walk around this stupid city and expect to get anywhere? Where the hell are the cars, trains...ANYTHING?"*

The people around Robert stopped without warning, causing him to stumble into the empty crosswalk. He caught his footing just in time to hear the blaring horn of a car coming from his left. It swerved past Robert and screeched to a halt in the middle of the intersection, and it wasn't long before the light bar on the roof flashed red and blue.

"*Great,*" thought Robert. "*Not even here a whole day and I'm already in trouble.*"

A well-dressed man stepped out of the car and pointed what looked like a gun in Robert's direction. Robert fought the urge to reach for his own pistol. He couldn't afford to make a scene in broad daylight.

"Sir, you are in direct violation of pedestrian safety law 26-2092: Improper Street Crossing," yelled the man. "Please identify yourself."

"My name is Le—"

"Don't yell it to me, sir. Roll up your sleeve and show me your identification tag."

Taken aback, Robert paused for a moment before lifting his arm and exposing the tag. A beam projected from the device in the man's hands and gave Robert's arm a quick scan. The man then holstered his device and closed the gap between them.

"I apologize for the rude behavior, Captain Smeebly," said the man, "but I wouldn't expect someone of your prestige to be walking around this side of the city."

Robert breathed a sigh of relief as the man came over and held out his hand.

"I'm Inspector Allen Devoe."

"Nice to meet you, Inspector," said Robert as he returned the handshake.

Robert could feel the suspicion in the Inspector's eyes as they studied Robert's features.

"I apologize for breaking the law, Inspector," added Robert. "I'll definitely be more careful in the future.

Unfortunately I have a very important meeting I must attend. You can just add that ticket to my file, and it will be paid immediately."

The inspector grinned as if he sensed Robert's urge to get away as fast as possible.

"I'll let you off with a warning this time, but I insist on letting me take you to your meeting. We'll cut the time in half by driving."

Robert could tell the Inspector knew something was strange, and the last thing he wanted was to spend more time with him in a car. But considering his long walk and his need to remain off the radar, Robert obliged and followed the Inspector to his car.

"I must say, I've never seen you at any of the gatherings in Zone 1," said the Inspector as they sped away. "Are you new here?"

"Yes," lied Robert, "I'm in the JHDF, but this is my first time in New Amsterdam."

"Well it's no wonder you ran into traffic. Here, put these on."

The Inspector handed Robert a pair of glasses, and Robert looked at them with reluctance.

"Don't worry, they won't bite," said the Inspector. "In fact, everything will make much more sense."

Robert slipped the glasses on and couldn't believe his eyes. The strange sheen disappeared and was replaced by a city full of color. Lights lined the street floors, and traffic signs floated in the air at every intersection. The signs above the storefronts and the flashing advertisements in their windows brought the once dull city to life. Robert even noticed one of the taller buildings had an advertisement for his favorite candy posted on its side.

"So that's what a Kaiser Bar looks like now."

"What did you say?" the Inspector asked.

"This place looks amazing, wow," saved Robert before changing the subject. "So does anyone else drive here? Where I'm from there are a lot more cars."

"Private transportation only exists for residents of Zone 1," replied the Inspector. "But for everyone else, there are buses and trains. Where exactly are you from?"

"The Republic of Texas," Robert replied. "The largest HIVE in the United States."

The inspector shot him a suspicious look as he slowed down and pulled to the curb.

"Right... Well, here's your stop. Phoenix Technologies."

"Wait a minute," said Robert, "how did you know I was going here?"

The inspector grinned.

"A JHDF member who has a very important meeting and is new to the city? You must not think I'm very bright."

Robert simply smiled and held out his hand.

"It was a pleasure chatting with you, Inspector."

"The pleasure is mine," he replied, shaking Robert's hand.

The inspector then pulled a plastic business card from his pocket and handed it to Robert.

"In case you ever need to talk."

Robert nodded and exited the car before watching it drive away.

"That Inspector could be an issue," he thought, *"but I should be fine as long as I keep myself under the radar."*

He stared down the street until the car went out of sight before turning to face his destination. Before him was a vast lawn in the endless sea of buildings. At the opposite end of the lawn stood the familiar tall building with a single spire. Red, orange, and yellow accents streaked along the flanks of the pure white building, lending no doubt to the company that built it.

"There it is. Phoenix Technologies."

Robert walked across the street to the sidewalk next to the lawn. As he got closer, he caught the distinct smell of plastic. The lawn which looked luscious and full from afar was fake and dull up close. Despite this, there were still signs staked in the turf which read 'KEEP OFF THE GRASS' in plain block letters. Robert chuckled at the senselessness of the signs.

"I guess they don't want to kill the grass," he thought.

He then looked up at the tower, only to focus on the space behind it. The sun floated high in a sky too perfect to be real. And even though the brightness hurt his eyes, he did not feel the familiar warmth caressing his face. The blue was full, but lacked true depth. As Robert looked closer to the tip of the tower, he could make out the waves of energy rippling from around the spire and radiating throughout the thin dome projecting the clear and sunny sky. As his gaze made its way back down the tower, he noticed the large advertisement floating above the entrance. The ad it displayed was for a Phoenix Technologies virtual reality device, but the screen soon changed to something much different.

The new ad had 'BEWARE OF THE BAD EGGS' sprawled in large letters at the top. Below it was a cartoon of a humanoid egg character. The gaping hole in the top of its shell dribbled yolk between its beady red eyes. The egg's hand held a wallet it recently stole from a man's back pocket. A big bird flew in the hazy red sky above the scene, giving an ominous feel.

The turf stopped about 100 feet from the tower's base where it met the concrete sidewalk. A few guards stood around the building's entrance, but that was no problem. He knew he could use the flow of the lunch crowd in and out of the building to look less conspicuous.

"Let's just hope this level 1 clearance pulls through," he thought.

He approached the door and flashed his wrist to the scanner. The door opened with a beep and Robert slipped inside.

And just like that he was in.

Robert entered to the echoing sounds of a talking crowd, and the clicking of heels against the polished slate floor. The expansiveness of the main lobby stretched up to a high ceiling that tapered to a dome above his head. Small seating areas and fake trees in jet black planters dotted the lobby. Behind the main desk in the center of the room stood a large, flat-topped pyramid made of gray marble blocks.

The polished stone glistened underneath the water cascading down its flanks. Perched atop this pyramid was the statue of a large bird with outstretched wings. The red, orange, yellow, and white granite slabs from which the bird was carved gave it the appearance that it was glowing with fire.

Robert noticed a phrase on the side of the pyramid as he passed the statue. Even through the running water he could make out the white marble letters inlaid in the pyramid.

"The Phoenix Gives Us Light.

The Phoenix Gives Us Life."

Robert ventured deeper into the lobby and found the line of elevators on the far wall. He waited until he could grab one for himself and slid in before the doors closed. Robert studied the display screen on the panel and scrolled until he hit the topmost floor. He made his selection, causing the screen to prompt for clearance. Another flash of his wrist gave him a green light, and the elevator juddered into a steady acceleration.

He watched the numbers above the door flash as the elevator sped past the corresponding floors. 10....30...50...90... At the 110th floor the elevator decelerated before coming to a halt.

"Floor 123: Executive Suite," announced a voice.

Robert stepped out of the elevator and into a white, well-lit hallway. He walked its short distance to the double glass doors at the end. The automated doors slid open, and Robert looked around to check his surroundings. A full-sized bar stocked with alcohol lined the left side of the room next to a lounge area in the far corner of the room. The room extended to the left behind the entrance, holding a pool table and an old bookcase. The right side of the room held a small bedroom blocked off by opaque glass, and a glass-faced desk sat at the opposite end of the door. Full-sized windows formed the outside walls, providing a bird's eye view of the city below. Enjoying the view was a woman standing in the lounge area. Her fiery red hair glowed in the midday sun.

"So one of the most wanted men in the city comes back," she said.

Decades had passed since Robert last heard Marcella's voice, but it still rang with the same confident tone. He paused for a moment to question the possibility of a trap, but he knew she would not be there if it were.

Marcella didn't seem to notice Robert's pause and continued to speak.

"Not only does he come back into the city, but he makes it into the Second Zone and all the way to the top floor of the Phoenix Tower. And he did this all without alerting a single patrol or civilian."

Marcella turned towards Robert and looked him in the eyes. She looked much older than Robert remembered, but she still looked at least twenty years younger than her true age. The skin on her no longer held the supple qualities of the young woman he once knew, but her thin nose still held a pair of glasses in front of her vibrant green eyes.

Marcella looked Robert up and down before cracking a grin.

"Looks like you still got it, Robert. But you didn't fool me, I saw you coming."

Robert laughed to himself. She may have been older, but it was the same old Marcella.

"Nice place you got here, Sis."

"Oh, you know me, Robert. Always need to feel comfortable when taking care of important matters. After all, it is *strenuous* work."

She took a sip from the tea cup nestled between her hands.

"So you mind if I grab a drink, then?" Robert asked. "After all, I should assume you didn't summon me here for any matter less than important."

"Oh, go right ahead!" she replied. "I have the finest stock in the city. I'm sure you'll find something quite satisfactory."

Robert went behind the bar and grabbed his favorite bottle of rum. Marcella shot him a nasty look as he uncapped the bottle and took a hearty swig.

"You know you could have just used the automated bar servant to get that, and you could have gotten a glass too."

"Ya know, it's more of a liability issue for me." He exhaled, making his way towards her desk.

Robert reached into his pocket for a cigarette, but the glare he received from Marcella made him change his mind.

"A glass is easy to poison," he continued, "but old-world alcohol is a commodity much rarer and more valuable than gold, or any other resource. Isn't that right, Sis?"

Marcella laughed and shook her head.

"Oh, I get it. You don't even trust your own sister."

"Hey, you can't blame me! You stood idly by while the council had their way with me."

Marcella shook her head in disagreement.

"What did you expect me to do, Robert? You blatantly disobeyed all your orders."

"I did the right thing!" he retaliated. "What did you expect from someone who worked behind enemy lines since before you were born? I followed my gut. I got the job done. I got everyone out of there."

Marcella looked at Robert with a cold stare.

"And then you managed to kill at least five guards, unlawfully cross multiple zone barriers, and leave the city without authorization. Not to mention the rest of your team faded into oblivion because of your mistakes. Joe was the only one with enough sense to make his amends."

Robert reached the comfy sofa chair around the coffee table and plopped himself down into it. He could argue all day with her, but knew it would go nowhere fast. He regained his composure and changed the subject to more pressing matters.

"Sit down, Marcella, and tell me for what joyous occasion you brought me here."

"I need someone with your particular set of skills to... run some *errands* for me," she replied.

Marcella sat down across from Robert and placed her cup of tea on the table in front of her. She paused for a second and then continued.

"You see, Robert, it is not often you find someone who can move around without attracting much attention, someone who can take swift action and disappear like he was never there."

"You mean like someone who only exists in the government's black book," Robert added.

"Now you're getting it. It's—"

"So what's in it for me, and why can't you do this yourself? After all, you are Governess of New Amsterdam."

Marcella looked at him for a second, hiding her frustration with his interruption behind a crooked grin. She took a sharp breath before continuing.

"You know how it is, *Brother*. Law under the HIVE charter states the individuals in question must be demoted in zone level, or shipped to Eisenstadt. But in this case, we need a permanent solution that's more....efficient."

Robert leaned back and crossed his arms.

"So you want me to just kill a bunch of people?"

"Among other things, yes," she replied. "And in return, I will give you your freedom. A new name, a new identity, and a new lease on life. And if you do your job well enough, I'll even give you a promotion. I'm sure you have some terms of your own, but remember that I can only do so much. I want you back, Robert. But if we fail to make an agreement here, I'll be forced to turn you in."

Robert met her glare and returned it, knowing that breaking the connection would lose him this battle of wits.

"You and I both know I'll take us both out before I let you turn me in," he replied.

He took a moment to collect his thoughts before continuing.

"No promotion. I want my amnesty, as well as permanent termination of my contract. Those are my terms. Given my service record prior to my *'mistakes'*, I believe I've more than earned it."

"Deal," she replied.

"Well then I should get started, shouldn't I?" he said, taking another swig from the bottle.

Marcella grinned.

"Now that's what I like to hear. I want you to spend some time getting yourself reacquainted with the city. I'll update you with your tasks in due time."

She reached inside the pocket of her pantsuit and handed Robert a wrist watch. It had a glass touchscreen, and the underside of the body held the Phoenix Technologies logo.

"What's this?" he asked her.

"It's a micro-computer," she replied, "It's time for you to modernize, Robert. This little beauty does everything your old unit does, and more. Not to mention it's half the size. Another ingenious invention from Phoenix Technologies."

"Another ingenious way of keeping tabs on me as well, no doubt," Robert added. "Do I even want to know how this thing works?"

Marcella laughed.

"Let's just say people are *dying* to wear it."

Robert placed the bottle on the desk, took the watch, and started towards the door.

"Not even a goodbye I see."

"Our business here is done," Robert replied.

He walked towards the door and stepped through the opening.

"Catch ya later, Sis."

He then disappeared down the hallway and into the stairwell next to the elevator.

Marcella sat in her chair for a couple of seconds shaking her head.

"Always needed to do things the fancy way, didn't you? Well, we'll see how long this lasts."

She stood up and took a swig from the bottle on the coffee table. As she turned around to look back out the window, she caught a glimpse of Robert's wing suit swooping down into the vast city below.

The sky almost disappeared behind the horizon, and only the occasional working streetlight illuminated the area. Old and decrepit buildings lined the streets. Many of their faces had missing windows, and showed signs of cracking under their own stresses. This part of town appeared abandoned, yet there were two figures walking down the street. They walked in silence until they turned into an alleyway halfway down the street.

"Is everyone here?" one of the figures asked.

"Everyone except you," called a voice from the shadows. "You're late, Julius."

Three more figures appeared from the depths of the alleyway to face Julius.

"Oh, quit your complainin'," Julius replied. "I needed to get our new recruit."

The figure who came with Julius still stood in the alley's entrance, but Julius grabbed him and dragged him towards the other three.

"I'd like you guys to meet Raj. Raj, this is Harry, Karen, and Ted."

Raj had a tan complexion, and looked to be in his late teens or early twenties. His lean, short body stood in contrast with all but Karen. Julius and Ted were burly and had an inch or two of height on him. Harry was much taller, but thin as a rail.

"Ah, so this is who you were talking about," said Ted as he shook Raj's hand. "You ready to show us what you got?"

"Yea," Karen continued, "we need to see if you got what it takes to roll with us. Nothing fancy, just distract until we get into place. We'll take it from there."

"Don't worry, I got it," Raj replied.

"Don't look too eager though, you don't want to blow it. One wrong move could put you in a serious world of hurt," Harry pointed out.

"Don't listen to him, you'll do fine," said Karen as she flipped her hair over her shoulder. "This part of the job is as easy as pie. I should know because before you came around, I was the one doing it."

"Yea but having a smokin' hot body definitely helps on your part," said Ted with a laugh.

Karen smacked Ted in the back of the head and gave him a scowl.

"I'm your sister, you idiot!"

Julius put his arm around Raj and interrupted their squabbling.

"He'll be fine. Good ol' Raj here puts in some good work at the junkyard. If he can do that, he's a shoe-in for this. And I've already prepped him for the job. We hide right by where those Zone 2 yuppies cross over to go to the bars, find an unsuspecting one, and take 'em for all they have."

Julius looked over his shoulder.

"Shhhhh, someone's comin'!" he whispered.

They all quieted down to hear the important news as Julius poked his bald head around the corner.

"Man with a long coat. No one around here dresses like that. He's definitely from Zone 2. But we're not anywhere near the bar so he must be lost."

At this point the butterflies began to build in Raj's stomach. He was not the kind of person to hurt someone, but the times had been tight. The junkyard didn't pay well and worked him like a slave. Desperation pushed him to the edge, and he was not looking to spend another night hungry. But most of all he wanted to belong. He had no one besides the people he worked for at the junkyard. While this rag-tag group may not be the best of friends for him, he yearned to have someone to call his family.

"Ok, you're up, kid. Now's your time to shine."

Julius gave Raj a little nudge towards the end of the alleyway. Raj stumbled a bit, but caught his footing just in time to not fall flat on his face. By this time the man had already passed the alleyway, so Raj needed to hustle to catch up. Every once in a while, Raj caught whiffs of a burning smell. It was very distinct, but also something he'd never smelled before. As he closed the gap between him and the target, the smell grew stronger. Raj could see the smoky trails emanating from an object pinched between the man's fingers. Mesmerized by the smoke, he closed in on his target and almost forgot the purpose of his mission. Raj needed to think of something quick to get his attention.

"Excuse me, sir," Raj called out.

The man kept walking as if nothing happened. Raj called out even louder this time.

"Hey, you!"

Still no reply, or even acknowledgment of his existence.

Raj didn't know what to say. Afraid of losing his big shot, he gave it one final try.

"Hey, asshole!"

The man stopped in his tracks, causing Raj to almost collide into him. He stepped around the man and saw his face for the first time. Raj froze as their eyes met. The man's blue eyes seemed to pierce Raj's soul, reading his every thought. He studied Raj for a second before speaking up.

"Whaddaya want, kid?" he asked in a raspy voice.

Raj had to think quick; it was his only shot.

"Please, I need help!" Raj begged. "My sister is back there and she can't walk. I need—"

"Let me make a suggestion to you," said the man as he cut Raj off.

He took a pull from the cigarette in his hand and leaned towards Raj as if to tell him a secret.

"I suggest you walk away and tell your buddies to back off. I know what you're up to, and trust me, you picked the wrong guy."

The look on his face was stone cold, and Raj could tell he was serious. But before Raj could say another word, the group appeared from an alleyway behind the man.

"Good job kid, we'll take it from here."

Julius stepped up to address the man.

"Give us what you got, and you're free to go."

"I was just telling your friend here about the mistake you're about to make," the man replied. "I'll give you one more chance to back off. After that, I can't guarantee a thing."

"So that's how it's going to be," said Julius.

Raj took a step back as Julius got closer. The stranger raised his hand to take another pull from his cigarette, but Julius smacked it from his hand.

"Gimme what you got, and we'll be on our way," repeated Julius. "This doesn't need to get ugly."

The man took a deep breath.

"Touch me again and it will."

Julius laughed.

"What are you going to do, huh?"

He approached the man and went to shove him into the wall, but this time the man sidestepped Julius' attack. In one swift motion he grabbed Julius' arm by the wrist and landed a forceful blow to the outside of this elbow. Raj heard the loud crack of breaking bones as he watched Julius' arm snap in an unnatural direction. Julius let out an agonized scream and dropped to the ground like a ton of bricks.

"BOSS!" screamed Karen, as she and Ted stepped in to join the action.

Ted got in close and swung his spiked club. The man ducked under his swing and caught Ted with an open palm upper cut to the jaw. Raj heard the sound of steel puncturing flesh and watched as the man's blow sent Ted's body flying effortlessly in his direction. Ted collided with Raj, knocking Raj down and pinning him to the floor with his lifeless body.

In his struggle to push Ted's large corpse off of him, Raj heard the thud of a body hitting the floor and the groan of someone catching a sharp knife to the gut. Julius' screams

51

stopped moments later, and the streets fell back to the silence of the settling dusk.

Raj could almost feel the footsteps coming towards him. He fought to free himself from underneath Ted with no luck. Suddenly the weight lifted off of him, and Raj found himself face to face with the man. The two locked eyes for what seemed like an eternity.

"Sit up," the man demanded.

Raj obliged, propping his body up from the blood-soaked pavement. The man lifted up the chest of his coat and reached inside with his right hand. Raj heard the clicking of a metal object.

"*Great, a gun,*" Raj thought. "*At least he's going to finish me off quick.*"

He closed his eyes and expected everything to turn black, but instead he felt something drop into his lap. Raj opened his eyes and looked at the object in his lap. It was a pristine pocket computer which looked like it had just rolled off the assembly line. Raj searched his brain for anything to say, but the man spoke before Raj could.

"This item is not for sale. It's definitely not a gift, and it's only yours for the time being. Should anything happen to it, you shall join your friends over there. Understood?"

Raj sat there and looked up at him in amazement. One minute ago he was fighting for his life, and the next, the crazed killer was almost befriending him.

"Understood?" the man repeated.

"Yes, but—" stammered Raj, but the man had more to say.

"Very good. There is a file containing a list of materials I will need you to get. If I wasn't already so busy, I would get them myself. You have forty-eight hours to get said items, otherwise...Well, consult exhibit A again. Understood?"

"Yes, but—"

Raj tried to speak, but the man cut him off once again.

"Excellent. I'll see you in forty-eight hours, give or take. And don't let that timer run out without you having checked off all the items. Your arm looks better when it's attached to your body."

The man turned to walk away but turned again to face Raj.

"One more thing. Get some real friends. Quit trying to hang out with bozos like these," he said, pointing at the sidewalk behind him.

The man then lit up another cigarette and disappeared into the night.

Raj had so many questions, but he could only manage to ask one.

"How will I find you?"

"Don't worry about finding me," the man called over his shoulder. "I'll find you."

The man walked another block and soon disappeared around a corner. Raj scooted himself over to the building so he could rest his back upon it. He took a deep breath and let it out slowly as he ran through his head what had just happened.

"What have I gotten myself into?"

He looked down at the wrist computer still sitting in his lap. The display showed two times. The current time, and a timer counting to his next encounter with the man. Raj slapped the device onto his forearm, causing the automated latch to close firmly around it.

"Well, it looks like I'd better get a move on."

CHAPTER 5: THE MIDNIGHT RIDE

The moonless streets were cold; much colder than Robert remembered. Hours earlier he'd arrived at his hideout inside the old Phoenix Technologies tower in Zone 5. Luckily for him, the building looked solid, and everything in his hideout remained untouched from the last time he left it. Perhaps there was nothing of value in there. More likely, it was inconspicuous enough to stay hidden. After all, Zone 5 appeared to be an abandoned wreck. The crumbling remnants of the old city looked akin to the cities Robert encountered outside the HIVE, making it blatantly obvious that decades had passed since anyone lived there.

But instead of wondering where it all went wrong, the more important issue brought Robert back to Zone 2. He crossed into Zone 2 to find a city unlike the one he saw earlier in the day. The massive crowds were gone, replaced by emptiness underneath the bright lights lining the streets. Even the advertisements and digital signs vacated their spots on the walls.

"I guess they all go to bed early on weeknights," Robert thought.

He continued down the quiet road until he found the garage where he'd hidden his bike. As Robert walked up the ramp of the garage, a security robot patrolled the well-lit streets. Its electric motor whined as it continued its patrol, but came to a stop by the entrance to the parking garage.

"Halt!" it commanded in its monotone voice. "You are in direct violation of the zone curfew instated under Amendment Thirteen of the New Amsterdam Charter. Surrender now, or risk termination."

Robert stopped in his tracks.

"Chances are I can't outrun this thing," he thought. *"I'm gonna need to take it out quick."*

He drew his pistol as he spun on his heels, ready to let the bullets fly. But Robert turned around to find the ramp behind him empty. He pointed his pistol down the ramp and waited for the robot to appear, but the shouting pleas of a woman rang out from outside the parking garage.

"NOO! PLEASE!" she cried. "I won't do it again, I swear!"

"Patricia Conlan. Aged 18. Place of Residence: Two Seven Five Old Mill Boulevard, Apartment Four," said the robot over the woman's whimpering.

Upon realizing the robot wasn't after him, Robert made his way up the ramp and towards the overhang to watch the scene below him unfold. The woman stood twenty feet from the drone, frozen in place as it inched towards her.

"This is your fourth offense pertaining to curfew," continued the robot. "Mental reconditioning efforts have proven to be unsuccessful. You will be detained and evaluated for possible reassignment."

"NOOO!" screamed the woman through her sobbing. "They'll send me to Eisenstadt! I won't go!"

She turned around and took off in a sprint. Unaffected, the robot pointed its arm towards the woman and shot a blue ball of light from its palm. She choked out a little scream as the ball hit her in the back and sent her diving into a skidding halt. The drone rolled over to her whimpering body and used its vice-like claws to remove her from the floor. It popped out a tray from its waist, threw the woman onto it, and disappeared down one of the intersecting streets.

"Well, that was close," Robert thought.

He wasn't aware of the curfew in the upper zones. It could have proven to be a fatal mistake, especially with ammo being in limited supply. Still, the close encounter had its benefits. It gave Robert a chance to study the drones without rousing too much suspicion. Their build seemed to be basic. Its two arms stuck out the sides of its metallic box frame, and the face was fitted with multiple sensors to allow it to perceive its surroundings. All of this sat on a large rubber ball. Robert guessed they may be easy to outmaneuver despite their strength in firepower.

Robert rounded a corner to find his motorcycle still sitting precisely where he'd left it. He mounted it and tapped on the gauge atop the fuel tank to make sure the reading was right. The needle on the gauge was just above the 100 psi mark, which was a little under a quarter tank.

"Let's hope this gets me back," he thought. *"It will be tricky, but I'll be fine as long as I don't attract any unwanted attention."*

Robert flipped the key on the handlebars and kicked the engine to life. Power surged through the bike, turning on all the center console lights and the headlamp. The low, buzzing idle echoed throughout the parking garage as Robert threw on his helmet and tightened the strap. After letting the bike warm up for a half minute, he pulled out of the parking garage and onto the street.

"It's been a long time since I've ridden on pristine pavement," thought Robert, *"but the bike definitely feels at home within these streets."* Within moments, his mind replaced the surrounding buildings with trees. The dull black sky filled itself with stars and a full moon. A woman in the seat behind him wrapped her arms tightly around his waist and whispered in his ear.

"Go faster, Robert."

Robert's wrist twisted the throttle, causing the motorcycle to accelerate down the road. An unexplainable sense of freedom came over him as the wind blew through his coat. Every bump, crack, and line on the pavement traveled through his tires and into his arms as he rounded the corners. The engine begged for more as it screamed under a fistful of acceleration. Robert's heart lived amongst the waltz of man, machine, and pavement as they intertwined through space and time. But just as Robert took his eyes off the road to look around, the moonlit forest dissolved into the quiet streets of the midnight HIVE.

"Oh, crap!"

Robert came to just in time to see the curbed patch of turf in front of Phoenix Tower closing in fast. With little time to think, he twisted the gas and popped the clutch. The front tire spiked towards the heavens, and in one swift motion, Robert threw all of his weight onto the handlebars. He pushed it with such force that the front of the bike sank and lifted the rear wheel off of the ground. The rear wheel clipped the top of the curb and sent the rear of the motorcycle upwards, but Robert regained control as it catapulted anchorless through the air. He came down almost sideways onto the grass, ripping two large skids across the otherwise pristine field. Robert fought to hold the slide until the bike caught traction and regained more forward momentum. It began to upright itself as Robert sped south towards the lower zones.

"That's not good."

Within seconds, a small aerial drone came flying overhead. It sank down directly above Robert and matched his speed. Robert saw the blue beam scanning him from above as it made its way towards the front of the bike.

"If this thing gets even a partial facial or retinal scan, I'll be marked as a high-priority target again," he thought.

Robert shrugged his shoulders and turned up his collar to hide as much of the visor as possible. He then drew his pistol and shot towards the drone. Two bullets were enough to send it crashing to the ground. Robert watched it tumble out of sight from the side-view mirrors.

He breathed a sigh of relief, but it was too soon. Flashing lights appeared in his side-view mirror as the security robots themselves flew down the street towards him.

"Well, here comes the welcoming party," he muttered to himself.

Robert twisted the throttle, and the bike surged hard with acceleration. The needle on the speedometer soon reached one hundred miles per hour, but the robots remained steady on his tail. They were so close, Robert could almost hear their monotone voices commanding him to stop.

"Time for some evasive maneuvering."

Robert grabbed a fistful of brake, sending one robot flying straight past him. He then turned left onto a side street, followed by a quick right to keep himself heading south. The maneuver pushed the bike to its absolute limit, but the old tires held long enough to get Robert safely through the corner.

He looked in his mirror to see one of the drones lose traction and tumble straight into the wall. It shorted out in a small electrical explosion, signaling the end of its pursuit.

"Two down, one to go."

Robert continued to accelerate down the street as bolts of energy whizzed past his head. He did his best to dodge and weave around them, even using the side-view mirrors to help him see. But as he looked forward, he saw the outline of a security bot roll out to the center of the street. Robert's heart dropped as his mind ran all the possible outcomes. None seemed to end well. But at a speed approaching eighty-five miles per hour, he needed to think fast.

"This better work."

Robert leaned the motorcycle into a slight left and waited until the last second to make his move. He then leaned the bike hard to the right, and then just as hard back to the left. The bike wobbled, but leaned just enough to squeeze right past. The robot in pursuit attempted the same move, but its wheels slipped, sending it tumbling into the robot blocking the road.

"These things don't know when to quit, do they?" yelled Robert as he saw another robot take chase. He pinned the throttle once more, but the bike lurched as if he'd hit the brakes. A quick look at the fuel gauge showed a mere 20psi left.

"Damn it, she's gonna die soon!" he thought. *"I only have one chance to take this thing out."*

He held the throttle steady through the coughs of the dying engine and fired his pistol down the street behind him. Some of his shots hit the target, causing an array of sparks. But the robot continued to return fire as it drew closer with every subsequent shot.

The bike gave one last cough as it exhausted the remaining hydrogen in the tank. Robert quickly pulled in the clutch and clicked the transmission into neutral. He let go of the handlebars, turned himself around, and fired away. The shots hit their target, but the robot shook them off as if they were pebbles being thrown by Robert's rear tire.

Just then, the gun's noise changed from hearty booms to gut-wrenching clicks. He reached for another clip, but at that point the bike veered heavily from the lack of speed. Robert turned back around on the seat and regained control of the bike. He locked up the back tire, and swung the rear end of the bike sideways. He allowed the motorcycle to high-side, and jumped off as it threw him upward. Robert soared through the air and landed on his feet in anticipation of having to fight with the mechanical beast. But when he turned around, there was nothing in front of him except his bike.

The security bot stood in place about fifty feet away as if a force field kept it from moving any closer. It still knew he was there, and watched Robert with its unblinking lens. Above the robot's head, a street sign hung over the middle of the road.

"You Are Now Entering Zone 2: Proceed With Care."

He couldn't believe his luck. Robert stood safe in Zone 3 as the drone stood menacingly within the confines of Zone 2, waiting for Robert to return.

"Not a chance in hell, my friend," he thought.

Robert holstered his pistol and picked up the motorcycle. He put it on the kickstand and checked it to make sure there was no major damage. Satisfied, he took it off its kickstand and rolled it away. He didn't get far before his wrist top let out its high-pitched ring.

"Hello," answered Robert as he accepted the call.

A familiar female voice came over the line.

"Hope you're settled in, Robert. I've got a job for you."

CHAPTER 6: THE FINAL COUNTDOWN

Raj woke up to the dreaded sound of his alarm buzzing. It normally meant it was time for a grueling twelve-hour day at the junkyard. But today, he had no intentions of going there. No, there was something much more important at hand.

Raj rolled over as he looked at the shiny new wrist top on his arm. The timer counted down from sixteen hours, giving him almost a whole other day to complete the task.

"I didn't find a single thing yesterday, which means I have to work even harder today," he said to himself. "But luckily I finally figured out how to use this thing." Raj pointed his wrist top at his alarm clock and pressed a button. A beam of white light scanned the alarm clock, bringing up pages of information on the wrist top's screen.

"Yesterday I didn't even know what half the things on this list were. But with this, I'll get everything in no time."

Raj stepped out of bed and onto the floor of his tiny room. He threw on the same old worn pair of jeans and smiled as he looked around his room. "This room might be small, and my fridge might be empty, but it's better than staying at the junkyard dormitory." The junkyard where he worked housed most of their workers, and his contract stated he needed to pay his monthly rent whether or not he slept there. Raj couldn't stay cooped up in that junkyard, but he also couldn't afford to rent an apartment in Zone 4. He found his happy medium in the back room of an abandoned store on the edge of Zone 5. It meant he needed to walk to work every morning, but to Raj, the freedom was worth it.

After throwing on a cleaner shirt, Raj grabbed his backpack and headed out the door. Now that he knew how to use the scanner, he decided it would be best to start his search in Zone 5. Although it had been slowly scavenged since its abandonment, its sheer vastness meant there must still be plenty to choose from. Raj made his way out into the bright sun, grabbing his pull-along wagon before heading through the towering remnants of decrepit buildings.

"I wonder what happened to this place," said Raj as he studied his surroundings. Buildings everywhere tilted as they crumbled under their own weight. Many of them were missing their windows, adding glass to the mix of rubble covering the streets. The shelves in the stores held odds and ends, but the apartments and homes seemed mostly untouched. It looked as if everyone had picked up and left

66

without warning. Raj didn't understand why they would leave all their belongings, but in this case it helped him a great deal.

"Now let's see here," said Raj as he looked over the list of items. Upon looking at the descriptions of the items he still needed, Raj realized most of them were readily available. An old cellphone, televisions, and other electrical devices were the main items on his list. But there were some hard-to-find items like lightbulbs and tools. It almost became a game trying to find all the items on the list. Raj learned so many things he didn't know before, like the purpose of this weird thing called a toaster, or a compact disc. Through his expansive searching and playing, and with the help of the scanner, he was able to find the majority of the items on the list except for two: A compressed air storage tank, and a working solar panel.

After searching throughout the day, Raj leaned up against a building and drank the very last drops from his canteen. "I've only got three hours left, but I still need a solar panel, and a compressed air storage tank." Raj thought hard about where he could find the items. But the more he thought, the more he came to the same conclusion. Raj put his hands on his head and stared down at the ground. "I have to go back to the junkyard," he said to himself. He paced back and forth on the sidewalk, arguing with himself. "No, I can't. I haven't been back there in days. What are they going to say to me? What am I going to say to them? I can't tell them what happened. They'll either call me crazy or punish me for trying to break my contract." Raj stopped

67

himself and took a deep breath. "No, I need to go back. It's either I face them, or face whatever awaits me at the end of this timer."

With his mind made up, Raj unloaded his day's catch within the abandoned store front and wheeled his wagon towards the upper zones.

By the time Raj made his way to Zone 4, he had less than two hours left. The mundane blue sky grew darker as the sun approached the horizon. Raj stared into the sky and thought about the recent events as he walked down the street. *"Just 48 hours ago I was trying to make a name for myself within the ranks of a gang. Now I'm fighting for his life. Scavenging items for a man and a purpose I know nothing about. I just hope I'm not as disposable as Julius and the others were."*

Raj continued down the street, keeping with the flow of people. The long walk to the junkyard caused the anxiety to build, but Raj looked around to try to keep himself distracted. *"Wow, there really are a lot of people,"* he thought as he looked through the crowd. Working at the junkyard meant waking up early and going home late, and he usually only ran into a few people during his commute. He never could have imagined crowds of people walking past the open store fronts. The smells of food wafting through the air replaced the usual bland smell of concrete and asphalt. Conversation and footsteps filled the normally silent void. Unlike the 'more work, less talk' ethic of the junkyard, people actually interacted with each other. It might not have meant much to the people around him, but to Raj it was a taste of the finer life.

Raj turned a final corner, causing him to gulp in fear. "Here we are," he said as he looked at the junkyard. The front entrance sat within a large wall of wreckage spanning across the width of the street. The rusted metal sign hanging above the gate had the words 'Ralph's Recyclables' written on it.

Raj approached to the banging and wailing of machinery emanating from beyond the wall. As he got closer he noticed the ice cream truck which made up the base of the wall. It stood next to the large closed doors, with the serving window on its side facing outward. A burly man with a long beard hung halfway out the window. He wore a white shirt underneath a pair of tattered denim overalls and held an electronic cigarette in the hand dangling out the window. It was Ralph Junior, and the sight of him at the front door made Raj's heart sink. Out of all the people who oversaw the work at the junkyard, RJ was by far the strictest. He once made a worker go all day without water because he took a water break without permission.

Raj tried to stay as calm as possible as he approached the window.

"Well, look who it is," called Ralph as Raj got closer. "Here to beg us for your job back?"

Raj swallowed the large lump in his throat and spoke. "I'm actually here to buy."

Ralph took a large pull from his cigarette and let out a berry-scented smoke screen.

"You've got a lot of nerve, Raj. Not showing up for two days straight and then showing up and expecting to get

69

in? I should hop out there and give you a whoopin' right now."

He shook his head before continuing.

"We found you lyin' in the streets. We clothed you, fed you, and even gave you a job. And this is how you repay us?"

"Please Ralph," begged Raj, "I wouldn't have missed work if it wasn't an emergency. I will be here tomorrow really early."

Ralph continued to study Raj as he took another drag.

"You're lucky I like you, kid. Otherwise you'd be coming to work with two black eyes on top of the two years we're adding to your contract."

Raj looked at him with dread in his eyes.

"What? No, please don't do that!"

"It's part of your contract. Want to make it five for insubordination?"

Raj dropped his head in defeat. Two more years on the contract was bad enough, he didn't think he could survive an extra five. Ralph merely looked at him with a grin.

"That's what I thought," he said. "Now get your ass back in here!"

A buzzer sounded as the gates crept open, and Raj slipped his way inside. The familiar smell of burning metal greeted him on the other side, making him shudder at the thought of being back. The main warehouse to his left and the living quarters to his right were the only buildings within the junkyard. Past that, mountains of scrap extended as far as the eye could see. A truck path weaved among the mountains, allowing easy access to the depths of the junkyard.

Raj stared down the path, not knowing what awaited him past the two buildings. It would be his first time going past the main warehouse and living quarters, and he didn't know what to expect. Raj took a deep breath before making his way down the path. He set his wrist top to active scan, and it pinged as it identified all the objects Raj walked past. Watch towers mounted with spotlights and guns dotted the yard, and Raj could hear the men perched inside making small talk as he passed underneath. It was an ominous reminder he was not the only one here. Any wrong move and he could wind up dead.

Out of nowhere, the pings from his computer became less sporadic and changed to three solid and repeating beeps. He checked the interface with excitement. Sure enough, *'Items of Interest Found'* flashed across the screen. Below the writing was a radar showing two dots. He ran towards the closest dot until he was right upon it. The object was a single solar panel about two feet by four feet in dimensions. Though it needed work, the computer determined it to be in working and salvageable condition.

"Perfect," he thought. *"Now all I need to find is this tank."*

The radar showed it was about a thousand feet away, so he threw the solar panel in his wagon and hobbled as fast as he could to the next location.

He rounded a bend around a tall pile of junk and came upon what he was looking for. It was an overwhelming sight. Hundreds of tanks piled on top of each other. Raj's heart sank as he looked at his wrist to see he only had 45 minutes left. He knew it would take time to find the perfect one. The instructions stated he needed one which would hold any fluid even if it were under pressure. He moved as fast as he could over to the pile and started ripping tanks from the heap. Rusted.....rusted...can't withstand pressure.... The scanning tool was hard at work deciphering the functionality of each. He finally found the perfect match with 15 minutes to spare.

"*It's all coming together,*" he thought. "*Now it's time to get them back.*"

He placed the tank next to the solar panel and wheeled them as fast as he could back to the front entrance. The straight path back got him there with only 5 minutes left. He placed the items on the checkout scanner, giving him the amount he owed. Raj smiled when he saw the amount of 675 credits flash across the screen. Raj had exactly 700 left to his name. He made it.

Raj put the items back on the wagon and dragged them over to the front gate. Ralph still sat there, billowing huge clouds of vapor into the air.

"You ready to go?" he asked. "We ain't got all day here."

Raj nodded his head. He finished catching his breath and dragged his loot to the front desk. Ralph peered over his counter at the items Raj had brought.

"Nice catch you got there," he said before inhaling another large puff. "That will be one thousand credits."

Raj looked at him in shock.

"What, ONE THOUSAND credits!? The machine said 675."

Ralph laughed as he looked down on Raj from his booth.

"You think I'd let you off the hook that easy? You *still* owe me, Raj. A week's pay for every day you were absent, and that's me taking it easy on you."

Raj put his hands together and looked up at Ralph with desperation.

"There's gotta be something else I can do for you to make up for what I'd owe."

"No can do. Cash only," Ralph replied, the grin still plastered on his face.

Raj looked down at the watch. Two minutes left. Panic set in as he frantically ran the options through his head. Steal the equipment and risk being hunted down like a dog, or show up emptyhanded and find out what's at the end of the timer. His heart raced so fast he could hear it smacking against the wall of his chest.

"Hurry up, we're closing soon," said Ralph. "Either you buy the stuff, or you bring it back where you found it."

Raj snapped back into reality and focused on the watch. 30 seconds left. Raj scrolled down on the watch and calmly checked off the last two items. The countdown stopped with 5 seconds to spare, and he breathed a sigh of relief at having stopped the immediate danger. He knew losing his arm wouldn't help him, but he also knew running away with the goods would be a surefire way of getting killed. Raj picked up the tank and the solar panel and carried them back towards the heart of the junkyard.

"Well, I guess it's time for option 3."

CHAPTER 7: THE WRONG SIDE OF THE TRACKS

Dreary clouds painted the sky gray, and a cold wind whipped through the forest. Stillness filled the gaps between the bursts of wind, but a strange humming sound replaced its grasp. It grew closer, adding a rhythmic clicking to the mix of sounds. A newly awakened squirrel pattered through the leaves on the ground. It hopped into the clearing of metal rails and froze. A reckoning force came its way, rumbling the very ground it stood on. Whether by fear, or simple forgetfulness, the squirrel moved out of the clearing just in time for the high-speed train to thunder through the forest.

The train ripped down the tracks until it climbed a section of rail that elevated it from the expansive forest below. Unknown to the operators of the cargo train, a stowaway hid amongst their ranks. He wasn't in one of the numerous freight cars, nor was he in the crew quarters as an undercover crew member. Instead, Robert Phoenix found himself strapped to the underside of the train.

"I really despise the cold," he muttered to himself as he put another cigarette in his mouth.

One click of his torch crisped the end to a fiery glow. After a deep drag, he released his breath and let the smoke fly past his face.

"*Of course I wouldn't be able to get in the train,*" he thought. "*Woulda sucked a lot less than this, but beggars can't be choosers.*"

So there he hung, watching the railroad ties whiz by his face. Like always, Robert had received a limited briefing. *'Get on the train and i'll let you know more when you need to know'* were his sister's exact words. Robert always hated when she did that. He could be heading into hell and not even know it. Luckily, quick thinking and cool-headedness were his specialty. Many adverse situations had molded him to be the way he was today. Where even the most battle-hardened soldiers would falter, Robert would remain collected. He knew there was always a way out, but his mind had to be clear enough to see it.

Suddenly his gauntlet vibrated, causing Robert to look at the screen. It was Marcella.

'Ahh, about time,' he thought before pressing the button on his earpiece.

"Checking to make sure I didn't run?" he asked.

"Cut it out. It's almost show time for you."

Robert grinned at his sister's serious tone.

"Relaaax! You know I'll get the job done. Speaking of which, what is it you're having me do all the way at the north end? It's cold. And in case you haven't noticed, I'm not exactly riding first class here."

Marcella laughed.

"Oh Robert, I'm glad to hear you're having fun. But now it's time to get your game face on. You've undoubtedly realized you are on a train heading north. In about thirty minutes, the train will reach the end of the line in the grand HIVE of Portland. Your objective is to make sure it *doesn't* arrive on time. In fact, the train must stop around ten miles outside the city limits."

Robert paused for a second before replying.

"Is that it, or is there something you are failing to tell me? One doesn't simply stop a train for the fun of it."

Marcella laughed again.

"Well you've got that right. But I hold the cards, and all you need to know is what I tell you. Nothing more, nothing less. If you do need some motivation, just know there may or may not be a bomb set to detonate when it reaches inside the city limits. You know how it is nowadays, Robert. Solid Intel is hard to come by."

Marcella took a quick pause before continuing.

"Well, it's time for me to get going. Catch you soon, Robert! Oh, and don't be late."

Without a moment's delay the transmission cut out, and his screen once again fell silent.

"Well this is bullshit," he muttered to himself.

If he'd remembered this would be the nonsense he'd be dealing with, Robert would've chanced running. It wasn't too late for him to leave. In fact, he was outside HIVE boundaries; miles from the nearest city state. He could jump train now and disappear before Marcella even knew he left. Robert looked past the train's wheels and off into the distance. The track sat upon tall pylons, giving him a view of a sea of slumbering trees stretching far into the distance. Even though the northern lands were still in the clutches of the dreary winter, he still saw the majestic beauty of the forest. It brought him solace to know he would once again return to its tranquility after this was over. At that thought he took one last drag from his cigarette and flicked it into oblivion.

"Time to get moving," he said to himself.

Robert turned around so his belly faced the floor of the cart above him. He unhooked his sling from the undercarriage and crawled upside down towards the locomotive at the back of the train. He was only a couple of cars away, but the journey seemed to take an eternity. His muscles burned from his struggle with gravity, but he continued to push ahead. Quick flashes of previous missions raced through his head, making it hard to keep his mind off the past. He thought he would never be doing this again. Yet, here he was hanging underneath a speeding train.

Robert stopped himself and took a deep breath. He knew the most important thing right now was to have his mind in the present. His mind focused on the wind rushing through his hair, and the rhythmic clicking of the wheels running over the tracks. The thoughts and worries trickled from his head little by little until the back of his mind's eye became a blank canvas. With a clear head, Robert looked ahead at the few cars remaining.

"Almost there," he thought.

Robert finally reached the locomotive and climbed into the gap between it and the last car. He rested himself on the catwalk and checked his wrist top. The map showed he had 12 miles until the stop point. He knew that would be just enough time to get the job done. Robert peered into the window on the locomotive's door to find a single armed guard on the other side.

"I need to do this quietly, but I also need to do it quickly."

He thought for a moment, but jumped into action as soon as he figured out a plan. Robert pushed against the walls of the adjoining cars and shimmied himself atop the roof. He then leaned down and knocked hard on the door. Sure enough, the guard opened it and quickly poked his head out of the passageway. After seeing nothing, the guard popped his head back inside. Robert waited a moment, and once again pounded on the door. This time, the guard walked out onto the catwalk to inspect where the noise came from. This was Robert's chance. He placed his hands on the edges of the two cars and straddled the gap between them. In one fell swoop he dropped into the gap and swung his body feet first towards the man. Robert's feet made solid contact, sending the guard tumbling off the platform and into the abyss below.

"Well that was easier than I thought."

Robert had to restrain himself from laughing out loud at the matter. Part of him couldn't help but find it humorous that this poor guy literally got kicked off the train. He didn't mean to make the guard the butt end of a joke, but that's just how it played out.

Robert lowered himself onto the platform and stepped inside the locomotive. The loud drone of the two large diesel generators greeted him as he entered. They lined both walls, forming a corridor with a door at the end. Robert wasn't sure how the guard had heard his knocking in the first place, but the lack of hearing ability made him proceed with caution. He crept his way to the door at the far end and slowly opened it. On the other side was the stark tranquility of the conductor's cabin. The control panel mounted in front of the leather bucket seats held numerous screens, knobs, and buttons. Strangely enough, both the pilot and copilot seats were empty.

"Huh, I guess these things are automated now," he said to himself.

Upon looking at the control panel, Robert realized he wasn't really sure how to stop the train. With only five minutes left to stop the train within the target area, he needed to figure it out fast.

"*I got this.*"

Robert took a seat in the pilot's chair so he could assess the panel, but he noticed something that sent chills down his spine. The seat felt warm to the touch. A warmth that could only mean someone was sitting there moments before. Robert hopped out of the seat and turned around to find himself face to face with the conductor of the train. It was a woman; not much shorter than he, with blonde hair tied into a ponytail underneath her hat. The business end of the handgun in her grip pointed directly at Robert's chest as she stood frozen in place.

"Thought it was strange there was no guard at the door," she said. "Now why don't you take a seat, Mr. ..."

"Lombardi," Robert replied.

He stood there for a moment while the woman eyed him.

"We both know that's not your real name. Now why don't you just go ahead and sit down," she said.

Robert took this time to get a closer look at her. The way she held the gun made it seem like she was uncomfortable with it, the situation, or both. The gun looked cheap in construction; almost as if it were a plastic toy. Robert was willing to bet they wouldn't entrust a conductor with a real weapon. It was all just show.

"Listen, you're right. That's not my real name. What you don't know, is you're way over your head on this one."

He motioned for her to put the gun down and continued.

"Now why don't you make it easy on yourself and put—"

POP!

Robert felt a sharp pressure on his chest as the conductor rushed in to subdue him. Still stunned by the unexpected shot, he almost couldn't react to her charge. His hands connected with her chest and he pushed her back as hard as he could. She went flying into the wall and dropped like a rock. Robert looked down to see her sprawled unconscious on the floor. He gave her a quick nudge to make sure she was out, and focused his attention on his wound. Robert noticed the small lead projectile stuck inside his coat and laughed.

"A pellet gun!? You can't be serious! How the hell do you expect this thing to do any damage?"

But as Robert pulled it out, he felt a sharp pain. It slid through the flesh as if the bullet had reached deep past his skin. Removing the pellet confirmed his fears. The pellet was a glass capsule with a syringe on its tip. Robert turned towards the control panel. His vision wavered, and he could feel his muscles starting to tense.

"It's a paralytic poison."

Suddenly he felt a huge weight on top of him, causing him to stumble backwards into the engine room.

"Gotya now!" the conductor said into his ear as she clung to his back.

He could feel the poison taking over as it became harder and harder to fight. Robert slammed her up against the wall as hard as he could until he felt her grip loosen. Robert then reached behind to grab the conductor, and tossed her over his head with all his might. She tumbled through the air and landed on one of the open generators. The current surged through her body, arcing bolts in a bright show of lights. This continued for a few seconds until the generator let out a loud pop. The whole room grew quiet under the loss of power, and the train slowed.

"Well thass wuhn way todo ih," Robert slurred.

He could feel his joints stiffening and knew he needed to hide before he could no longer move. He looked around and saw nothing. Nowhere safe. He stumbled back into the cabin and closed the door before his legs finally failed him. Robert fell over and landed on the floor with a solid thud. Despite his inability to move, he remained conscious. All he could see was the floor beneath him, and the wall to his side.

"So this is how it ends," he thought.

But he knew it would not be the end. They would sentence him to live in Eisenstadt once they revealed his true identity. He would become a part of their game; a fate much worse than death. So there he waited. No choice in the matter. No longer in control of his fate.

As the train came to a halt, Robert heard voices enter the car. They were yelling. Screaming. Though their exact words were muffled by the wall between them, Robert recognized the panic in the voices. Gunshots rang through the air, and it became clear to Robert he wasn't the only unwanted guest on the train. But who was this other mystery person?

It sounded as if they were waging full-out war outside that door, and Robert was just along for the ride. Bullets ripped through the wall next to him as the two parties exchanged fire. He listened to the guns cease one by one until there was nothing left. The car door at the back of the locomotive slammed shut, followed by footsteps on the metal floor. The clanking of boots on the metal floor grew louder as their wearer treaded closer. The figure took three quick steps before kicking the door open.

There was a pause before the footsteps thudded into the room. Robert would soon find out who this mystery person was, for better or for worse. The footsteps stopped right next to him. Robert could feel the stranger's gaze piercing him as the man stepped over him to look at Robert's face. The clicking of old cell phone buttons filled the silence, followed by a conversation in Russian. The man continued to talk on his phone as he poked and prodded Robert to make sure he was alive.

"Great," thought Robert. *"If there's anyone who hates me more than my fellow countrymen, it's the Russians."*

The conversation continued for another minute before the man hung up the phone and knelt down next to Robert.

"You are a lucky man," he said, switching his language to English. "Normally my orders do not favor the weak or misfortunate. You would be killed or left to die."

Robert could hear him digging through his satchel and placing items on the floor next to him.

"Russians don't show pity, especially for American agents. But since you helped me, I will help you. Consider this a thank-you for buying my ticket into the HIVE."

Robert felt a sharp pain in his shoulder. Cold fluid rushed through his arm as the man administered what Robert assumed to be the antidote. The man got to his feet and walked towards the door. Just then, Robert's wrist top rang sharply.

"You should probably answer that," said the man before disappearing back into the hallway.

Robert could feel the antidote slowly taking effect. His muscles loosened, and he struggled to move his free hand towards his wrist top. After a minute, the antidote freed his muscles enough for him to answer the call.

"Good job, Robert. You completed your objective, but you can't stick around. A train heading back to New Amsterdam will pass your train in ten minutes. Board it and get back to me..... Robert? Are you there?"

"We have a greater problem now," Robert grunted. "A Russian agent managed to get aboard and infiltrate the HIVE."

"That's all right, we'll get him," she said, dismissing Robert's concerns.

"We need to take him out!"

"Those aren't your orders, Robert. Have you already forgotten the cost of insubordination?"

She continued talking, but Robert stopped paying attention. How could she not care about this? Even more important, how could he allow himself to get taken down by an amateur? It panned out, but it was too close of a call. But none of it mattered now. It was time to get back to New Amsterdam.

Chapter 8: The Third Option

Almost a week passed since encountering the mystery man, but the events of that fateful night still ran through Raj's mind. Part of him felt bad for the others, but another part of him was happy he survived. More concerning was the emptiness from a lack of concrete answers. Who was this guy? What was his story? And what was Raj's role in all of this? If Raj had known, maybe he wouldn't be sitting in the back of a flatbed truck filled with scrap.

On his way home from the junkyard a couple nights ago, he'd thought long and hard about how he would get the last two items. Showing up emptyhanded wasn't an option, and stealing them in broad daylight was suicide. But as if by luck, he'd stumbled upon the most fascinating device. It was two long tubes tied together that made far-away things look closer. His wrist top called it binoculars, but Raj liked to call them the tubes. Messing around with the tubes gave him an idea. He could watch the guards at night and find a way to get in and sneak the parts out undetected. It was a risky move, but it was Raj's best chance. So for the next couple of days, Raj showed up to work as promised. He toiled through the laborious day of smashing old car batteries and sorting through all the junk which made it into his pile. But when the sun fell, Raj did not go to sleep like all the others. He instead spent his nights in a building with the best vantage point of the junkyard.

Though he wasn't able to see the junkyard in its entirety, Raj was able to determine a general routine. The guards changed post at midnight, and seven in the morning. Although the gates closed at sundown, there was a covered flatbed truck which always came in near midnight. The changing of shifts, and the lax attitudes of the midnight crew played in Raj's favor. His only problem was getting back out. There were a few scrap mountains near the fence he could climb. It didn't look easy, but he had no other choice at this point.

So Raj sat inside the scrap-filled truck, waiting to slip into the junkyard. His heart raced as the truck closed in on the gates. Almost every ounce of his being yelled at him to get out of there. That last ounce, either courageous or suicidal, told him to see it through.

The truck squeaked to a halt, causing its mass to sway on the suspension. Raj then heard two voices yelling over the growl of the truck's idling diesel engine. They talked for a minute before the slamming of the truck door once again shook the truck. The voices grew louder as Raj's heart pounded in his chest. Soon he heard voices emanating through the opening in the back of the truck.

"What you got back here?" one voice questioned. "You're about one hundred pounds heavier than your ledger says."

The flap on the back of the truck lifted up and a bright light shined upon the heaps of junk. Raj tried his best to duck away and hide himself while not drawing any attention.

"The usual I suppose," stated a second voice. "Old technology and other salvageable metals. The scale we have is probably off. It's gotta be twice as old as I am."

The first man lifted himself up into the back of the truck and looked around with his flashlight. Raj's heart felt like it might explode at any moment. He was done for! The light crept closer, followed by the silhouette of the man. The beam of light came inches from Raj's face, and Raj closed his eyes and prepared for the worst.

"BEEP BEEEEEEP!"

The truck's horn sounded loudly, causing both Raj and the figure to jump in fright.

"Jenkins, that bastard!" said the man with a scowl. "He's going to get 'randomly selected' for the cavity search next time."

The man hobbled out of the truck and yelled swear words as he made his way back towards the cab. Raj let out a sigh of relief.

"That was close," he thought. *"I never thought I'd be so thankful for jerks."*

After about a minute of muffled yelling, the truck once again lurched forward. It wasn't a smooth entrance, but he was in. Despite his nerves still going haywire, Raj guessed it was safe for him to come out. He wedged himself out from the debris and crawled to the back of the truck. They had just passed the first guard tower and were heading deeper into the yard.

"*Almost there,*" he thought.

Raj saw the second guard tower pass by and jumped out soon afterwards. He didn't expect the speed of the moving truck, and his legs were not enough to keep him from smashing hard onto the floor and tumbling to a stop. It didn't take long before the pain shot through his right shoulder, making him well aware that it had taken the brunt of the impact. Raj tried his best to shake it off and assess his surroundings. Confident his presence remained unknown, he set off the short distance to his stash point.

Raj closed in on the stash point and gave the items one final scan. 'Working Condition' flashed across the screen of his wrist top.

"*Perfect,*" he thought, "*we're good to go.*"

Pain once again jolted through his shoulder as he attempted to throw the panel on his back. Raj dropped to his knees and clenched his teeth to keep himself from screaming in agony. Giving up and retreating crossed his mind. He would be lucky to get out of there at all with his shoulder in its current condition. He thought about pretending to have fallen asleep in the back of the truck. Maybe they would let him out alive. It was tempting, but the little voice inside his head egged him on.

"If you don't die here, you'll die out there. Keep moving, you can't stay here!"

Raj took a few deep breaths before once again throwing the panel on his back. His shoulder screamed at the thought of lifting his arm above his head, but he pushed through the pain. After balancing it on his back, he found a length of extension cord to secure it around his waist. Raj grabbed the compressor with his good arm and headed towards the edge of the yard.

But just as he crossed the truck path, the glow of flashlights moved down the path in front of him. His heart raced as he looked for another route. None of the nearby ones were short enough for him to hide around a bend, and hiding behind a scrap pile would make too much noise. He panicked as his mind ran through the options, but suddenly the clear and obvious answer hit him.

"I'm wearing junk, so I can look like junk! Brilliant!"

At that instant he planted himself into the closest mound and waited. It wasn't long until one voice came within hearing distance.

"You know, it's nonsense they have us out here. I mean, look at this place. It's a freaking fortress!"

"Oh quit your complainin', you're gettin' paid to do nothin'! I would love to sit home and watch 'The One Zoners' but I have mouths to feed."

"You should get that TV recordy thing! What's it calle....."

The voices faded once again, and Raj continued on his way. As he looked back to ensure there was no one behind him, his foot caught a hard object sticking up from the floor. Raj stumbled and tried to run it out, but it was no use. He soared through the air and landed belly up on one of the piles. The crash of the impact was followed almost instantly by an encore of crunching metal. A broad section of the mountain came cascading downwards, blocking the path behind him in an avalanche of aluminum and steel. It barely missed Raj, who lay still strapped to the solar panel like an upside-down turtle. He struggled to right himself, but managed to tip himself over and get on his feet. His ears still rang and his shoulder seared with pain, but the lights reflecting off the mountains coming ever nearer caused only one thought.

"*Run.*"

Raj darted off in the opposite direction, making an all-out break towards the fence. His body screamed at him, demanding him to stop. It was reaching its absolute limit, but the one thing he couldn't do was stop. Raj heard voices from behind, so he weaved in between mountains in an attempt to lose them. The tank grew heavy in his arm and his lungs burned with pain, but he ran as fast as possible until he reached his final obstacle.

The tall fence ahead was the only thing separating Raj from freedom. Though the piles next to it were much taller, Raj now saw they weren't close enough to make the climb any easier. He looked up with dread at the razor wire curling around the top of the fence. It would have been a remarkable feat for someone in perfect condition, let alone with a busted shoulder.

Raj felt trapped.

"There has to be another way," he thought.

He looked around but saw nothing. The fiery pain engulfing his shoulder made it unbearable to move. Defeat trickled into every ounce of his being. He untied the cord around his waist, dropped the compressor, and sat down against the fence.

He was done.

There was no helping him. There was no changing it. He fought well and gave it his best, but it was not enough. Raj just hoped they would get it over with quickly.

The voices were getting nearer, meaning it was only a matter of time before they found him. He was losing his focus, zoning out of the real world. But a clear voice called out from behind.

"Get up, kid. Time to go."

Raj turned his head to see the very man who'd sent him on this quest plugging away at his wrist top.

"C'mon! How does this damn thing work again?" he said with frustration.

Raj sat there in a daze, wondering if his mind was playing a trick on him.

"Ah Ha! Now I remember."

The man pointed his arm at the fence as a red laser protruded from his wrist top. He then moved it in an arc around Raj, causing the fence behind him to fall away. Raj followed it, groaning in pain as he slammed against the floor. But before he could say anything, the man grabbed him by his shirt collar and dragged him backwards a couple feet before heading back into the junkyard.

"C'mon kid, get up! You're no use to me as dead weight."

Raj fought through the pain to get himself onto his knees, and watched as the man returned with only the compressor.

"The... the panel," said Raj, fighting to not stumble on his own words.

"It's broken," the man replied.

He scooped Raj underneath his armpit and lifted him to his feet.

"Let's go."

"And where do you think you're going?" rang a familiar voice.

Raj looked up at the shadowed outline of Ralph Junior standing about thirty feet in front of them. His hand clenched tightly around a baseball bat with sharp metal welded to it.

"Who's asking?" questioned the man as he squared up to face Ralph.

"The owner of the establishment you just stole from," Ralph fired back.

The man looked at Ralph with curiosity.

"Ralph Junior then, is it?"

"The one and only."

The man smiled to himself.

"Well, that's funny, I have a package specifically for you."

The man reached into his coat pocket as if he was looking for something. Ralph did not like the man's apparent sarcasm and headed towards the pair with his bat at the ready. Barely strong enough to stand, Raj could only watch as Ralph closed the gap.

"Don't think you can sweet talk your way ou—"
BANG!

An intense ringing filled Raj's ears as he looked over at the smoking barrel of the gun resting in the man's hand. He then looked back at Ralph's lifeless body on the floor in front of them.

"Got some of the low-hanging fruit out of the way," the man muttered.

He continued to talk to himself as he holstered his pistol and typed on the screen of his wrist top. But the yells echoing from the junkyard grew closer, and the man once again dragged Raj along with him.

"Now we really have to go!" he yelled.

Raj stumbled after the man, but he couldn't keep up. The man kept looking back and yelling at Raj, but the words were indistinguishable. Raj's legs gave out from under him, and all went black.

CHAPTER 9: THE MAN BEHIND THE COAT

It was mostly a blur. Small flashes of alleyways and side streets. Tiny snippets of Raj answering questions he didn't remember. The next thing he knew he was lying on the floor of a dark room. Raj tried to move, but his body remained frozen to the ground. Suddenly, a light appeared from above, and Raj saw the outline of a figure standing above him. He spoke to Raj in a deep, calm voice.

"Find the key. Escape the darkness. Embrace the unknown."

"What?" asked Raj.

Those vague words could mean anything. But instead of clarifying, the figure repeated himself.

"Find the key. Escape the darkness. Embrace the unknown."

"Who are you, and what does that mean?" Raj cried, still attempting to wrench himself from the ground.

The figure continued to look down at him.

"Those are the steps. If you follow them, you just might find out."

The figure walked away as the light from above zoomed towards the floor. Raj took a sharp breath and sat straight up, only to find he was no longer in the dark place. In fact, he wasn't sure where he was at all. He was on a cot in the corner of a small, windowless room. A single light hanging from a wire above illuminated what appeared to be a bedroom. It reminded Raj of his small room, but this room definitely wasn't his. He took a moment to collect his thoughts, going back to the dark place he'd just left. It was all a bad dream, it had to be. He woke up in the room immediately after the light, but it all seemed so real. Raj tried to think past that. Running was the only thing he remembered.

Raj slipped out of bed, but felt a tug on his arm. He looked down at his left forearm to see an IV needle buried under the skin. Panicked, he went to pull it out with his free hand. But as he did, he felt a sharp pain and soreness in his shoulder. The memories hit him all at once, and the fear sank in.

"I have to get out of here!"

Raj ripped the needle out of his arm and bolted towards the door. He forced it open and stumbled into the other room, but stopped at what he saw. Tables, desks, and shelves lined the walls and formed corridors throughout the large room. Items ranging from glass jars to computers filled their spaces, but their conditions captivated Raj the most. They were all things Raj normally found broken and forgotten in Zone 5, but everything in this room appeared untouched by the destructive forces of the rest of the HIVE. It was almost like stepping back in time.

A voice calling from the other end of the room drew Raj's attention.

"Was wondering when you were going to wake up. It's already been three days."

Raj turned around and saw the man at a table on the other side of the room. The welding goggles covering his eyes reflected the intense light emitted by the welder in his hands. Raj couldn't see what he was working on, but the glow of the welder radiated across the room.

"Who are you?" Raj asked as he crept toward the man.

"Me?" replied the man without looking up. "I could ask you the same. You've got either a lot of balls or a death wish going into a place like that and expecting to make it out in one piece."

"Well I had no choice," Raj argued. "It was die by your hand, or die by theirs."

"How are you so sure I would have killed you?"

"Wha wha...." Raj stammered.

He couldn't believe the words coming out of the man's mouth.

"You took out a whole group without breaking a sweat, threw me a wrist top with a timer on it, and hinted towards it blowing up! What are you, some kind of juggernaut jokester?"

The man stopped welding and laughed to himself.

"I have been called many things during my lifetime, but that one is a first."

He lifted the goggles off his face and looked towards Raj.

"I prefer Robert."

Robert pulled a cigarette from his pocket and stuck it in his mouth.

"Besides," he added, "I wouldn't blow up that wrist top. That's how they've been keeping tabs on me. Well, at least until now."

Raj was at a loss for words. He couldn't decide whether to be mad about what he went through, or to be glad it was over. But before he could say anything, Robert continued.

"You are free to go. You held up your end of the bargain, and I am grateful for you doing so. Oh, and by the way..."

Robert picked up the new wrist top from the bench and tossed it to Raj. He caught it and juggled it in his hands until he found a spot to hold it that didn't have a hot bead of weld.

Raj still couldn't figure this guy out. Was he an enemy? A friend? Or, perhaps a bit of both. Regardless, Robert intrigued him. Robert could fight and stand up for himself. He was the exact opposite of Raj, who wasn't able to fend for himself in most situations. Raj knew he would have a much easier time surviving if he knew how to fight like Robert. On top of that, Raj felt this strange connection to him. He didn't know why, but he had the feeling he had been waiting for a very long time for Robert to cross his path. So Raj built up enough courage and spoke.

"Could you train me to be like you?" he asked. "You know, how to fight and stuff?"

Robert laughed, taking another drag of his cigarette.

"You really want to be like me, kid? You're the first person I've heard say that in decades."

"So is that a yes?" Raj asked excitedly.

"Definitely not."

Robert stood up and walked across the room towards another table.

"To know what I know would take years, maybe even decades of training. It's definitely not something I can teach you in a short time, especially not here."

"Well how did you learn it?" Raj asked.

Robert shrugged.

"The hard way, mostly. Along with the uncanny gift of being difficult to kill."

Robert turned his attention towards a shelf and rummaged through its contents. Raj walked over to him in an attempt to be more persuasive.

"I'm a quick learner," he insisted. "And you don't have to teach me everything. The basics will work."

Robert chuckled to himself.

"Well I must admit, kid, you're stubborn as hell. And you have potential to boot."

Robert grabbed a knife off of the shelf as he spun around to face Raj. The event happened so fast, Raj didn't have time to react to the sharp blade now pressed against his throat. Robert looked Raj dead in the eyes as if studying the contents of his soul. Raj returned the stare, albeit shaken by the knife on his windpipe. He didn't speak out of fear the knife would slit his throat, but rather left Robert to fill the silence.

"The first and most important rule is to always expect anything and everything. Instinct can be a much greater asset than even the most thought-out plan."

Robert removed the blade from his throat, and Raj pedaled backward to put some distance between the two. Robert once again turned back towards the shelf before continuing.

"With that being said, a clear and open mind is crucial. It could mean the difference between life and death."

Robert placed the knife back on the shelf before picking up a ball and tossing it to Raj.

"Think fast!"

Raj put all his focus on catching the ball, failing to notice Robert rushing towards him. By the time he realized his error it was too late. Robert closed the gap and placed one of his legs behind Raj. He then grabbed hold of Raj's shirt and forced him backwards. Raj lost his footing but Robert's firm grip on his clothes kept him from crashing to the floor.

"Rule number two is to always be aware of what is happening around you."

Robert pulled Raj back to his feet before continuing.

"It is rare that things will happen one at a time because everything is constantly changing. You need to be in harmony with your environment. Be one with the wind blowing in your face, and every single rain drop hitting your skin. Always in the moment."

"Wind.... rain..." Raj murmured.

They were words he had heard before. They sounded magical, almost mesmerizing. But then it hit him where he heard those words before. It was from the old beggar who would sit outside the junkyard at lunch. She always told these elaborate stories of the world outside the walls. Wind, rain, a real sun. Plants and animals. Most people didn't take her seriously. No one was allowed beyond the wall because no one could survive. Life was only possible within a HIVE.

Nevertheless, Raj always found her stories fascinating. Just the thought of a whole world out there, let alone a survivable world. The woman always talked about it as if she had been there. Raj believed there had to be some grain of truth to them, but most thought her stories were merely to score money for food. But now Raj knew it must be true. A man so young looking as Robert had spoken of those things as if they were known to all.

"You're.... you're from out there, aren't you?" Raj murmured.

Robert was taken aback by the question.

"Yes, yes I am."

Robert gazed across the room. He hadn't even been in the HIVE for two weeks, but he already missed the tranquility of his old life. He would give anything to be back around a campfire cooking a fresh kill.

"So it's true, there really is life out there!" Raj exclaimed. "Oh, how I've imagined exploring beyond the wall. It must be fascinating! Tell me, Robert. How is it?"

Robert still gazed off into the far corner of the room.

"As dangerous as they say, but more beautiful than you can ever imagine," he answered.

"I knew it! It's always been my dream to go outside the HIVE."

He started to dance around in joy but then stopped to face Robert.

"Have you told anyone about this yet? You can show them the world isn't a wasteland anymore, and then we'll be free to go back out there!"

Robert snapped out of his gaze and looked at Raj.

"You're a bright kid," he said, "but you've still got a lot to learn."

Robert extinguished his cigarette in a nearby ashtray.

"Lesson's over, kid. See ya later."

Robert turned around and went back to looking through the contents of the shelf. Raj grew flustered, but wasn't going to give up that easy.

"Well tell me what it is I should know."

Robert didn't bother glancing around at Raj.

"Maybe some other time, kid."

This frustrated Raj even more.

"But how—"

"Don't make me kick you out, Bernard," said Robert, cutting him off mid-sentence.

'Bernard?' thought Raj. 'How could he mix up my name that badly?'

But he realized he'd never told Robert his name. Raj walked towards the exit and stopped before passing through the doors.

"The name is Raj by the way."

With no response from Robert, he continued on his way out. He approached the doors to the outside as they swooshed open. As Raj crossed the threshold, he realized he was inside an abandoned building. File cabinets and desks were upended, their contents strewn across the floor. A stale air with an old and almost foul smell hung with the darkness in the room. It was as if a storm had rushed through the area and no one came back to clean it up.

The doors behind him hissed to a close, and Raj turned around to see nothing. The doors there moments before were replaced by a wall with the same disheveled facade as the rest of the room. But then Raj caught a whiff of fresh air coming from one of the broken windows. He followed it through the corridor of cubicles until he was face to face with the broken window. Raj gasped as he looked down upon the HIVE below. The lights of all the zones shined brightly under the night's sky. He could even see the Phoenix Tower off in the distance. The colored streaks which ran up its sides reflected light like a beacon for all those who could see it. It was a wonderful view. Raj strained

105

to look past the reaches of the HIVE, but his vision past the wall was obscured by some kind of haze. He yearned to know what it was like beyond the walls.

His thoughts were interrupted by a rustling behind him. Raj turned around in time to see a larger figure coming in his direction. Taking a cue from Robert, he ducked out of the way and towards the middle of the room. It was a boy about Raj's age, with a heavy build.

"C'mere!" the figure yelled, turning around to barrel towards Raj.

Raj dodged him again, this time throwing in a punch that glanced the figure's face. Pain seared through his arm, reminding him of his current condition. But even a half-strength punch was enough to illicit a reaction from his foe.

"Yeaooww!" yelled the figure as he stumbled around. "That's it, you're toast!"

Raj didn't stick around. He darted off in the opposite direction, sprinting through the cubicles until he found a door with an exit sign above it. He ripped it open to find two more men and a woman on the opposite side. Raj nearly tripped as he backpedaled away from the door.

"Ah, what have we got here?" one of them asked.

They poured into the room towards Raj. The one chasing Raj closed in from behind and joined the others to form a circle.

"Found him up here alone. I think he's what the Major is looking for."

They circled Raj like sharks. He thought about yelling for Robert but knew his attempts would be futile. He tried to remember back to how Robert handled the situation the first night he met him. After all, the situation was quite similar. Raj took a deep breath and tried his best to sound confident.

"Leave me alone, o-or you'll be sorry!"

They all chuckled.

"Got a feisty one here!"

One of them lunged towards Raj, but Raj ducked his advance. Another closed in on him, and Raj threw a defensive punch with his uninjured arm. She dodged the punch, allowing her to land a direct hit to Raj's ribcage. The fierce blow knocked the wind out of him, causing Raj to fall to the floor in a struggle for air. The sounds of laughter echoed in the background. All he could focus on was the pain reverberating through his chest.

Suddenly he felt the sharp impact of a foot to his back. Raj arched backwards in agony as he fell to the floor.

"HELP! ROBERT!"

He prayed Robert would hear him and come to his rescue, but his cries for help went unanswered. The one Raj had punched closed in with revenge in his eyes. He raised his foot high above the ground, and Raj had no choice but to close his eyes and brace for impact.

"ENOUGH!"

The voice cut sharp through the air, and they all fell silent. Raj heard the footsteps coming closer. The voice spoke again.

"Get up," it commanded.

Raj loosened up and opened his eyes. Standing before him was something unexpected. It was a gorgeous young woman who also looked to be around Raj's age. Black boots adorned her feet, and dark cargo pants hung from her waist. Her dirty blonde hair was tied into a ponytail behind her tight black shirt. Raj obliged her as quickly as possible, struggling through the pain to get back on his feet.

"Name?" she prompted.

"Uhhh Raj," he replied, taken aback by her commanding presence and beauty.

"Age?"

"Twenty?" he guessed.

"Well, Uhhhhraj," she said, "what is it you are doing up here?"

Raj looked around thinking of a quick excuse. Even if he told them the truth, it was a fat chance in them believing him. Raj took a breath and continued.

"It's just Raj. And I was up here to look at the beautiful view. You can see the whole world from here."

Raj pointed to the window he was looking out of just moments before. He expected her to look towards the window but she did not. Her eyes remained glued to his shining wrist, almost transfixed by it.

"Right." She nodded. "And where did you get that?"

Raj's heart felt ready to burst from his chest. He looked down at the wrist top and examined it for the first time since he got it back. It had a shiny metallic band and body. The interface was still in pristine condition, and despite the welds Robert made, it looked seamless.

"This old thing?" he asked. "I found it with some junk and cleaned it up to look nice."

Raj's glance met hers, and it felt like she could see right through his lie. They held the glance for what seemed like an eternity.

"Ok. Stay out of trouble," she said as she turned away. "Let's go, squad, he's not what we're looking for."

They all turned and filed in behind her. Although Raj was happy to skip another confrontation, it felt too easy. On top of that, they were just as mysterious as Robert. Maybe they were allies. They might even be sworn enemies. Whatever the truth may be, his curiosity drew him to them.

"Who are you guys?"

The leader turned around to face him.

"You wanna know who we are?" she asked.

She walked over and bumped her wrist top to his.

"We'll have a meeting soon. Expect to have some info forwarded to you."

She turned back around and disappeared through the doorway with the others. Raj sighed and pressed himself up against the wall. He stared into the darkness of the room, trying to replay in his head what had happened.

"This is what you get when you want to be adventurous."

Chapter 10: Old World Blues

Several weeks passed since Robert had last heard from Marcella. He spent most of the time taking stock of supplies, creating a system to generate and store hydrogen for his motorcycle, and cutting his beard and hair to a more manageable length. The rare downtime from his chores was spent reading the book he found at Phoenix Manor. Robert thought it was a good read.

It was about an elf wrongfully put in the prison of a mythical land. The elf needed to break out, but found the prison to be inescapable. But one day, the elf realized the only way to get out unscathed was through the most obvious place: the front gate. All the elf needed to do was create a distraction and find the key. So the elf waited until the gatekeeper was on the other side of the jail and broke into his office. It was there he found a spare key wedged in between the pages of a book. The elf then put together a plan and slipped out by the skin of his teeth.

But even a good read wasn't enough to keep Robert's mind off his mission on the train. Who was this Russian agent? What was his business inside the HIVE? And the most important question – why didn't Marcella flinch at such a high-profile security breach? The unsettling feeling that Marcella had something to do with this put finding an alternate route out of the HIVE higher on Robert's priority list. Even without the possibility of a Russian collusion, Robert didn't trust his blood ties with Marcella would keep him safe. She was still a business woman and a politician. And if there was one thing Robert knew, it was business and political deals were neither exclusive nor transparent.

With little ideas, Robert headed out to check his original escape route. It was located in the sewers on the northwestern fringe of Zone 2. Luckily, Robert did not have to navigate miles of tunnels like he had on his last go-round. With his clearance restrictions lifted, he no longer needed to worry about getting caught in Zone 2.

BING BONG

"You have now reached the end of the line at Pearson Park. Please exit the monorail."

The car doors slid open, and all the people inside the train filed onto the platform and down the stairs to street level. Robert stood up from his seated position and stretched his arms and legs out wide.

"It would be nice to actually ride inside the train one of these days," he thought, *"but it isn't worth using my ID chip.*

For all I know, Marcella could be using that to track me too. The last thing I want is her wondering why I'm snooping around Zone 2."

He waited for everyone to leave the train before he jumped onto the platform and walked down the stairs. The city in this part looked very similar to how it did in the past, and it wasn't long before Robert found a familiar alleyway with an entrance close to his tunnel. Robert lifted the cap and lowered himself into the sewer. To his surprise, waist-deep water greeted him at the bottom.

"Well that's not good," he thought.

The water level at this part of the tunnel during his last escape barely reached above his ankles, and even that time he still needed to swim underwater to make it outside. With the water this deep, Robert feared it would be almost impossible. Despite this notion, he decided to push forward. He waded about 100 feet towards a fork in the tunnel and took the left fork to where the exit tunnel should have been. Instead, there was a wall of concrete rubble blocking his path.

"Now it makes sense why there's so much water," Robert muttered to himself.

The exit was one of a few drainage points positioned around the city, but was the only one Robert could safely escape from. If the HIVE walls could not keep out the rough seas, or groundwater otherwise penetrated the system, these exits let the water return to the outside world. The collapsed tunnel created a dam, stopping the water's exit to a mere trickle.

Robert stared at the rubble dam standing before him and thought through his options. He would need some serious power tools and a lot of time to clear up this mess. Neither of which he had. Robert was discouraged, but far from admitting defeat.

"Where there's a will, there's a way," he thought.

He brainstormed ideas as he waded back out of the sewer. His options weren't all that plentiful. Even if he made it through the initial blockage, there was no way of guaranteeing the rest of the way would be clear. The tunnel could be collapsed anywhere within the mile-long crawl to freedom. The train leading out of the HIVE was the next best idea. Unfortunately, his recent escapade had caused them to tighten train security for the unforeseeable future. It would not be impossible, but by no means would it be easy.

Two options Robert noted were blasting through the outer wall, or climbing over it. Needless to say, blasting a hole through thick concrete would not be subtle, and would also require large amounts of explosives. On the other hand, scaling the wall would be less conspicuous, but making it through the atmospheric membrane may prove to be a challenge. The only sure-fire way to get through was to power it down, but that meant turning off the most mysterious part of the city—the power source. Robert laughed at the irony of his situation. The only thing known about the city's power source was it worked without fail. The only person with the knowledge to create and control it was long gone.

Robert finally reached the sewer cap and climbed back up to street level. He then pulled a cigarette from his coat pocket, lit it, and filled his lungs with the familiar burn.

"Old man really knew how to build an impenetrable fortress. The only surefire way in and out is..."

His jaw dropped with his sudden revelation, but the sharp ring of his wrist top brought him back to reality.

"Ah, my favorite sister. How's it going?" said Robert, answering the call.

"Oh Robert, you flatter me. I have more business for you to take care of. Unfortunately, I also have a lot of work in the upcoming months, so you will receive all future orders from my associate."

A deep voice with a commanding presence came over the line.

"Welcome back, Agent Phoenix. I am Commander Aesculus — Senior Delegate of the American Republic Intelligence Agency, and top advisor to The Honorable Marcella Phoenix."

Robert scoffed at Marcella's title before taking another drag of his cigarette.

"Nice to make your acquaintance," he replied. "I don't mean to be that guy, but let's cut to the chase. My time is precious."

The commander cleared his throat.

"Very well then. We've got some targets for you to take care of, all of which rank high on our watch list."

"So hold on," Robert interjected. "If she's got ARIA backing her, then why bring me in?"

The commander sighed with frustration.

"I thought your time was precious, Mr. Phoenix. The why of it doesn't matter. You're not a citizen; you're not even a soldier. You are property. The only thing that matters is what we tell you. And if you want your freedom, obeying our orders is exactly what must be done."

Robert's blood boiled. He clenched his fist into a tight ball and prepared himself for the piece of his mind he was about to unleash. But before he could let his words fly, Aesculus continued as if all was well.

"The list has been uploaded to your wrist top. As you finish one, another will take its place. Better get started, your time is precious."

The transmission cut out as Robert exhaled in frustration.

"*I see Marcella still surrounds herself with jerks,*" he thought. "*But I guess that just comes with this line of work.*"

Robert took one last pull of his cigarette before he flicked it down the street.

"*High-priority targets require intricate plans, and intricate plans require the proper equipment. I could try to ask Marcella, but I don't think that will go well. Even if she did give me something, it would most likely be shoddy equipment that couldn't be traced back to her. I need to find someone who I can trust that also has dependable equipment.*"

Robert knew it was a long shot, but he had one person in mind who might still be around: Nelson.

❖

A couple hours and several miles later, Robert found himself in the streets of downtown Zone 3. Brick, stone, and rusted steel buildings painted by the afternoon sun stood in rows along the avenues. The faded lines on the pavement served as another reminder of the world before. Despite the old world being long gone, the city was not.

The people heading to their destinations filled up almost every inch of sidewalk. Vendors selling all types of goods lined the middle of the unused roads. Some of the intersections were even filled with large, circular buildings made of whatever scrap materials could be found. Robert caught whiff of all the foods as he strolled through the streets. He could hear the banging of pots and pans intertwined with the sounds of talking, laughter, and footsteps. The heart of Zone 3 was alive. It felt as if Robert had stepped back in time. The nostalgia of walking these streets almost engulfed him, but he kept his head. He knew business came first.

Robert walked a bit longer before stopping in front of a store on the corner of 5th and Broadway. Iron bars rested within the window frames, and the neon sign above the door which once read "Lucky's" now only flickered the "LU's". Robert opened the door to the nostalgic ring of a physical bell hanging in the frame. Inside the store, he found the shelves and refrigerators barren. A middle-aged woman with graying hair sat behind the register. She looked over at him with distrust as he appeared through the doorway.

"Buy or get out," she said.

Robert unfastened the top buttons of his coat as he walked over to the counter. Without hesitation the woman drew a revolver and pointed it at his head.

"Get out."

She looked him dead in the eyes as Robert returned the stare.

"I'm here to see Nelson," he replied, raising his hands in the air in front of him.

Robert approached with caution and pulled back his collar to expose the tattoo on his neck. The ink had faded with age, but the two Greek letters of Delta and Omega still stood out against his light skin. The woman pulled him close and pressed the pistol against his throat as she inspected the tattoo. Satisfied, she let him go and pressed a button underneath the counter. A metallic sound emanated from Robert's left, and a section of the wall swung open to reveal a passageway. Robert gave the woman a nod as he left the counter and entered the opening.

He followed a staircase downwards into a dimly lit room. It was complete with a lounge, pool table, and a small bar next to a large glass humidor. But the main feature was the desk towards the back of the room. It was neat and simple, with one small desk lamp fixed to it. Behind it was a comfortable leather chair facing a television on the back wall. The news was on, but the volume was low enough to make the words indiscernible. A thick haze hung over the area, and the smell of cigar became stronger as Robert approached.

"Ghosts," said a voice. "They linger around without sound. Whisper in your ear and bring fear. Keep you up at night even though they're out of sight. Yet, you know they are there. How is that?"

"Because those who you can see have seen," Robert replied. "Those who you can hear will whisper of their doings. And because those who know all did not know what they saw or heard. Ghosts. Th—"

"That's all we are," the voice finished.

The chair spun around to reveal the man occupying it. He had dark skin, short gray hair, and a stubbly salt and pepper beard. His warm brown eyes matched the grin his lips cracked around a smoldering cigar. The man studied Robert for a second.

"You aged well, Brother," he said. "It has been a long while, yet you look exactly as I remember you."

"You're not looking too bad yourself," replied Robert.

They both reached out and grabbed each other's forearms in a symbolic handshake.

"It looks as if you are enjoying retirement quite nicely," Robert continued.

Nelson chuckled.

"Definitely can't complain."

He let go of Robert and leaned back in his chair before continuing.

"So Robert, what can I do for you?" he asked.

"I'm just going to come out and say it. I need guns, ammo, and any other supplies or gadgets that might prove useful."

"C'mon Robert, you know those are hard to come by."

Nelson paused to ash his cigar and looked back at Robert.

"Besides, I'm officially retired now. Don't have the government hookup I used to."

Robert looked around the room as he returned Nelson's volley.

"Yet here we are in a windowless basement that is impenetrable by imaging or listening technology."

Nelson took a lengthy drag from his cigar before changing the subject.

"Tell me, what brings you back to the HIVE?"

"You know I wouldn't come back for any other reason," Robert muttered with disgust.

Nelson looked at him with interest.

"Ah, so you *are* working. Why come to me?"

"Because I know you'll have everything I need to get the job done," Robert replied. "And because I know better than to think Marcella would trust me with a gun, or any other weapon."

Nelson laughed as he took another puff.

"You've got that right. Giving you a long-range rifle wouldn't be smart on her part."

Robert could almost see the gears turning in Nelson's head as he thought out his next move.

"I'll tell you what," Nelson proposed. "You can have full access to my inventory under two conditions. The first is guaranteed protection when the hit finally gets placed on my head."

Robert grinned.

"And the second?"

Nelson returned his grin as he gave the second half of his proposal.

"I need you to retrieve something for me."

"What would that be?"

Nelson made the tip of the cigar burn bright red and filled the air with smoke.

"The U.S.S. Obama will dock in the lower shipyard tonight before heading up to Zone 1 in the morning. One of the things it is carrying is a payload of Warhammer missiles. I need at least one of the guidance system chips out of those missiles."

Robert was taken aback at how uneasy the request made him feel. Why would Nelson need the most advanced guidance system known to man? Or even worse, whom would he be selling it to?

"That look you're giving me tells me you're unsure of my intentions," added Nelson. "I can't tell you what I'm using it for, but you'll have to trust me when I say you won't regret it. Just like I trust I won't regret making this deal with you. After all, I'm the one asking you to steal from the very people you work for."

Robert considered the consequences. If he got caught, he was dead. But he needed this connection to get supplies. And then there was Nelson. He was a bit strange, but Robert knew him well. When Nelson said something, he meant it.

"Consider it done," he said, shaking Nelson's hand.

"Excellent," replied Nelson. "Lucinda will have a package ready for you upstairs with some equipment you may need for the operation."

Robert nodded and walked towards the exit, but Nelson called for his attention once more.

"One more thing, Robert. If you ever find yourself a free agent, there's always a high-ranking position for you within my organization."

Robert shook his head.

"You know I prefer to work alone, but I'll consider it."

Nelson laughed.

"You haven't changed a bit. I'll see you soon."

Robert ascended the staircase back into the shop to find a backpack already waiting for him on the counter. The woman smiled and nodded as Robert slung the strap over his shoulder and pushed into the outside world. The sun dipped below the horizon, and the streetlights buzzed above the crowded streets. Robert lit a cigarette and looked at the sky. There was something about the night that just felt right. Robert wasn't sure what it was, but he knew where he had to be. He used his wrist top to figure out his bearings and mapped a route to the U.S.S. Obama.

"Looks like I'm going fishing."

CHAPTER 11: THE GHOST SHIP

It was an average night in the HIVE. The sky held the same monotonous shade of black, and the streetlights illuminated the area with their familiar yellow glow. But tonight was special, Raj could feel it. The surrounding air buzzed with good vibes. After all, it was the night he was to meet with The Major – the mysterious young woman he met nearly a month before. When he woke up this morning, he found a message sent to his wrist top.

Raj,

Meet me at the corner of New Amsterdam Ave and River Street at midnight tonight. There is something important I need to show you.

The Major

Raj wondered what the big thing was that she wanted to show him. He even wondered if there was anything to show at all. Perhaps it was a date; a chance to get him all alone. Between Robert and the mysterious girl, Raj's head filled with more questions than answers. He hoped some of them would be answered tonight. So there at the corner of New Amsterdam and River Street, Raj waited for his secret rendezvous. He even showed up early to make sure he didn't miss her.

The first thing he noticed upon reaching his destination was the colossal ship docked in the water across the street. It was unlike anything he had seen before. The gray painted sides were adorned with a large white 23. The top of the ship was mostly flat except for a large structure sticking upwards from the middle of the ship. With the ship docked parallel to the street, Raj could fully gauge its sheer size.

As he marveled at the vessel, Raj caught some movement out of the corner of his eye. On the other side of the street, a figure watched the ship from down the road. The figure's dark clothes blended with the night, and Raj probably wouldn't have noticed the figure at all if he or she had been a few feet farther from a working streetlamp. Raj's heart pounded. In a completely deserted street, that person could only be The Major. Raj crept across the street towards the figure. As he got closer, he realized the person lurking in the shadow was not The Major. Instead, he ran into the person he least expected to see.

"Robert?"

Robert turned around and motioned for Raj to be quiet.

"Jeez kid, could you be any louder?" he said in a low voice.

"Sorry, I just wasn't expecting to meet you here."

Raj's cheeks blushed at the embarrassment of his mistake, but he regained his composure.

"Say, what are you doing here anyways?"

"I could ask you the same question," Robert shot back.

Raj noticed that Robert's gaze never strayed from the ship in front of them. Before Raj could press the question again, Robert changed the subject.

"She's beautiful, isn't she?" he said, pointing at the ship. "I remember when she was first commissioned. Those were the good old days."

Robert cracked a small grin as he reminisced.

"She's old technology now though. Nuclear powered. Could you imagine that?"

"What do they run on now?" Raj asked.

"Who knows?" Robert replied. "Sebastian Phoenix created the Phoenix Core long ago, but the Phoenix Technologies database wiped itself as a failsafe to being hacked just days before the patents became government property. If they had those, any new ships would run on core technology."

Robert's eyes lost their focus as he looked back into the past.

"The world would also be a much different place."

He took a drag of his cigarette and brought the conversation back on track.

"They tried taking one apart once. Damn near took out a whole city with the explosion."

Raj was just about to ask him how he knew all of this, but Robert changed the subject once again.

"So you still want to be like me?" he asked.

Thrown off by the question, Raj could barely hold in his excitement or answer the question with coherent words.

"Uhb-duh yea!"

"Perfect," Robert exclaimed.

He took one more drag on his cigarette and flicked it into the water.

"I need to get on that ship."

"Wait, what?" Raj asked in disbelief. "That one? Why?"

"Need-to-know basis, kid," said Robert, dismissing his question. "Now are you going to help me, or not?"

Raj sighed in frustration, cueing Robert to continue instructions.

"I see you still have my fancy wrist top. Good, cuz you're gonna need it. You're also gonna need to take this."

Robert handed Raj a cylindrical device about the size of a can of soda.

"What is it?" Raj asked.

Robert smirked as he patted him on the back.

"Your next lesson."

He looked around to make sure the coast was still clear before turning back to Raj.

"The question is this: If you do something, and no one was there to witness you do it, did it even happen?"

"Well..." Raj began, but Robert cut him off.

"Rhetorical question," he sighed. "The point is, stealth is your best friend. Conflict is a last resort, so it is always best to use every possible resource to avoid it. And for tonight, you are my resource."

"Ok...." Raj said, still trying to piece out how he fit into the picture. "Oh, you mean this!?"

Raj shook the device in front of Robert, causing Robert to grab his arm in panic.

"Be careful with that! That thing is at least fifty years old. Who knows what will set it off."

"Sorry!" Raj whispered again. "So what do you need me to do?"

Robert pointed to the front of the vessel.

"I need you to go over to that side of the ship. When I tell you to, you pull this pin and throw the cylinder onto the deck."

"That's it?" Raj asked.

"That's it for now," Robert replied.

Robert hoisted himself atop the railing and looked down at Raj.

"Hope you have a good arm."

He then took one step forward and plummeted into the abyss. A few seconds later Raj heard a barely audible splash. He slid over to the railing and looked down to see nothing but a thick darkness below. Not a moment later, his wrist beeped. Raj looked at the screen only to see the words

"Incoming Call" flashing across it. He'd never gotten a call before, but assumed the green button was the right one to press. The beeping stopped, only to be replaced by splashing noises.

"Hello?" he whispered.

"Are you gonna sit there and stare, or do what I asked you to?" asked Robert in a labored voice. "Time is of the essence, kid."

"Oh-oh, sorry," Raj apologized.

He turned in place and strode towards his position.

"You are insane by the way," Raj added. "That was a tall jump. Even with the water I would have been scared."

"When you get to be my age, you'll realize there is no sense in fear," Robert replied in between breaths. "It is only your mind's illusion of what could happen, not what will."

Robert once again changed the subject.

"I'm almost at the deck. Are you in position?"

As he took his final steps towards the bow, Raj looked at his wrist top to check the time. He saw he still had a half hour until midnight and breathed a sigh of relief. He did not want to miss his meeting with The Major. He almost became lost in his thoughts, but the sound of an annoyed Robert brought him back to the present.

"Here now," whispered Raj.

"Good," exclaimed Robert. "Now let's take a look-see."

Raj imagined him peeking over the lip to survey the deck of the ship, and it didn't take long for his mind to wander once more. How exactly did he get onto the ship?

Were there stairs, or even a ladder? It would seem out of place on a ship so massive, but then again, Raj had never seen one so massive before. And even if there were a ladder or stairs, you would think they'd be guarded. Raj was about to ask when Robert's voice rang out over the radio.

"We're clear, kid. You're up. Take your time with the throw. The second you confirm it hits the deck, go find cover in the shadows."

Raj looked at the cylinder in his hand, examining it for the first time. It was surprisingly heavy for its size. Inscribed in faded yellow paint was the code "M18" in large bold letters. Robert's voice once again came over the radio, snapping Raj back into reality.

"You there, kid?" he asked

"Yea," replied Raj, "throwing it now."

He stuck his finger through the loop and ripped at the pin. It took some force, but Raj broke it free from its tight slot.

"Well, here goes nothing."

Raj took a little crow hop and threw the device skyward with all his might.

"C'mon, go!" he whispered to himself.

The seconds felt like an eternity as he watched the faint outline of the canister descend until it clipped the very edge of the deck.

Raj's heart sank. He listened in panic for the splash but heard nothing. It was so silent he could hear the buzz from the street lamps along the street. Instead of hearing a splash, Robert's voice echoed through the speaker.

"Did you throw it?" he asked.

Raj's heart throbbed in his chest. It would be devastating to tell Robert he failed him. Raj stuttered in his attempt to tell him.

"I...I..."

BANG!

Raj stumbled backward as the explosion caught him by surprise. He looked at the vessel, only to see an enormous cloud covering the front half of the deck. The relief that flooded him was stifled by the sounds of sirens and voices. Despite this, Robert's voice came calmly over the speaker.

"Well, that wasn't supposed to do that. Definitely worked though. Nice throw, kid."

"What's going on up there!?" Raj asked.

"Calm down, kid," Robert assured him. "It's only a minor setback. But stick to the shadows in case they look overboard."

Raj's head swiveled around, looking for a suitable spot to hide. The street lights lit up all his surroundings except for a small alleyway across the street. Not seeing much choice in the matter, Raj snuck his way into the dark alley. From there Raj continued to watch the havoc unfold, all while listening to Robert talk to himself.

He wondered how Robert could be so calm in a situation like this. What had he done to make this seem like it's a walk in the park? It made Raj's mind wander once again.

"He was from the outside world, so what was he out there? Maybe he was a great adventurer who traveled far and wide, facing many dangers. Or maybe even a soldier in the HIVE army. But if he was a soldier why would he need to sneak onto the ship?... Is he an enemy soldier?"

Raj was once again brought back to reality by the sound of Robert's voice.

"All right kid, I'm at my objective. How are things looking above ship?"

Raj peered over to see the smoke dissipating from the deck.

"The smoke is starting to clear," he whispered into his wrist top.

"I guess I'll have to move quickly then," replied Robert. "Needed that smoke to move everyone on deck. Makes—"

Robert's voice abruptly stopped, causing Raj to grow worried.

"Robert.....Robert! Are you there?"

Raj waited a couple of seconds, but still there was no reply. His mind swelled with the thoughts of all that could have happened. Captured... killed.... dead battery. But as abruptly as it had left, Robert's voice came back over the airwaves.

"There's someone else down here," he answered in a hushed voice.

"Well grab what you need and get out of there!"

"No, no. Something doesn't feel right. I'm switching you to visual."

"Wait, what?" Raj thought. *"Switching to visual, what does that mean?"*

He was about to ask just as his question was answered. The wrist top projected a screen showing Raj exactly what Robert saw.

Robert was crouched amidst a catacomb of large cylindrical tubes neatly stacked on one another. As the camera peered down the space between them, Raj caught his first glimpse of the figure. The light cast him as a shadow sticking out of the organized corridors, and his clothes hid the lines of his frame. Robert changed cover to get a better view. The figure was without a doubt a man. He knelt next to one of the cylinders with his hands outstretched into an open bag.

"What is he doing?" Raj murmured to himself.

"Don't know," Robert replied. "I'm going to grab the package and get out of here."

Robert turned to the cylinders, but stopped in confusion.

"What the..."

He flipped open the already broken access panel door and probed around inside.

"It's gone!"

Robert began flipping open all the access panels on the nearby tubes. Nothing. He then returned his attention to the figure. The figure was standing now, pressing buttons on his wrist top before opening one of the access panels on the tube in front of him and yanking a computer chip from inside. Robert snuck behind the figure and rested the muzzle of his pistol at the base of the man's skull.

"Don't move," Robert commanded.

Robert then noticed the man was making a call on the wrist top.

"Hang up now if you value your life."

Without a single word, the man lifted his free hand toward the wrist top and ended the call. Robert then continued with his demands.

"Good. Now give me the chip."

The man stood motionless and remained quiet. Without hesitation Robert pulled back the hammer on his pistol.

"Do not make me ask again."

The man opened his right hand to show his compliance. He reached into his pocket and pulled out a chip which rested snugly between the thumb and pointer finger of his closed fist. Robert grabbed the chip and placed it into his own pocket before questioning the mystery figure.

"Who sent you?" he asked.

Silence.

Robert was about to push the figure when Raj saw the man's right hand open up.

Clink clink... BANG!

An enormous flash of light filled the room, causing Robert to yelp in pain.

"Robert, are you ok!?" cried Raj.

No reply.

The camera came into focus to reveal a sideways picture of an empty room. Robert groaned as he scuffled to his feet.

"That was a textbook mistake, kid. I'm clearly still a little rusty. But hey, I got what I came for."

The camera panned all around the room and fell upon the bag the figure was previously digging into. Robert walked over and peered into the bag's innards. It was full of wires tied into an analog clock.

"Raj, you need to run and take cover."

Raj was confused.

"Wait, what? What is that?" he asked.

"Remember that thing you threw on the deck?" asked Robert. "Well picture that times one million."

The camera panned and headed towards a nearby doorway, but gunfire from the hallway greeted Robert almost immediately. He ducked to the side of the opening and fired back with the machine pistol he had buried in his coat.

"Run, kid, get outta here!" he yelled in between shots.

Before Raj could say anything, the screen disappeared back into thin air.

"Robert....Robert!"

Silence.

Not even a single crackle rang through the speaker on his wrist top.

"Damn it!" yelled Raj.

He peeked out of the alleyway towards the ship. The constant wail of the siren masked the yells of the men who still scrambled along the deck like ants. Raj sprinted towards the rear of the ship and jumped onto the railing. He didn't see Robert amongst the crew members scurrying along the deck. Raj scanned the street and the water, but Robert was nowhere to be found. Raj's mind told him to stay and help Robert, but his gut told him to listen to Robert's orders. He stood and looked at the carrier for a moment, unsure of what he should do. Then Robert's voice rang clearly in his head.

"Always trust your instincts."

Without hesitation Raj turned on his heels and took off in the opposite direction. He ran, not knowing or caring when to stop. He only made it 100 yards before it happened.

The sky lit up in a fiery explosion, followed by a giant shock-wave that threw Raj to the ground. The windows of the surrounding buildings burst from the force of the shock-wave, causing glass to rain down like razor-sharp hail. The silence turned into a deafening ring as Raj's body began to comprehend what had just occurred. His body screamed with aches and cuts, and he felt the familiar wetness of blood pooling on the ground below his face. He felt weak, but he knew he couldn't rest.

"C'mon!" he yelled as he coaxed himself to his feet.

With his sense of balance failing him, Raj turned back towards the dock, only to see a fiery glow in the distance. He tried to run, but could only stumble towards the light. The alleyway guided him like a chute, keeping him on track as he bounced between the walls. Raj's jaw dropped at the sight awaiting him beyond the alley. The entire rear section of the ship's hull had disappeared, replaced by an inferno consuming the rest of the boat.

Although Raj could still not hear or walk correctly, he tried his best to look for Robert. He found it to be a futile attempt, but needed to know if Robert had made it out alive. He called out for Robert as he weaved between the twisted metal, flaming debris, and bodies littering the streets. The smell of everything burning made him sick, and his body grew weaker.

"I need to find him," he thought. *"He got out alive, I know it. But he might need my help."*

Raj tried to push through the pain, but he looked at his arms as they glistened a bloody red in the light of the flames.

"I need help."

His head began to spin faster as his body grew too weak to balance. But just as he was about to fall to his knees, an arm swooped in to grab him.

"Robert," Raj murmured.

His vision faded, and once again all went black.

CHAPTER 12: THE ORDER REVEALED

The cold ground chilled Raj's back, and a musty odor filled the air. As Raj regained his senses, he realized he was once again pasted to the floor below a blinding light.

"C'mon Robert, knock it off," called Raj.

"I'm flattered, but I am not Robert," replied a familiar voice.

It took a second, but Raj remembered the voice from the first dream.

"You!" Raj yelled into the abyss. "Who are you then?"

"I could ask the same of you, Raj," replied the voice. "I could answer that question, but I believe you can't even answer that question about yourself."

Raj's blood boiled.

"What is this? How do you know me? Why am I bound to the floor?"

The man laughed.

"Oh, but are you really bound to the floor?" it asked. "Take a good look and tell me what it is that holds you."

Raj peered over to see his bare arm lying on the concrete floor. There were no chains, or any sticky substance keeping it in place.

"Nothing," stated Raj.

"Exactly," replied the voice. "Your mind is the only thing keeping you in chains. Free it, and free yourself."

Suddenly the force holding Raj's body disappeared, and he lifted himself to his feet. He looked around but didn't see anything within the swath of light around him. The voice called again from beyond the light.

"Do you remember the steps I told you?"

Raj paused for a moment. He had questions more important than remembering the steps.

"Yes, bu—"

"Name them."

Raj huffed, but knew getting this out of the way would get him closer to his answers.

"Find the key. Escape the darkness. Embrace the unknown."

"Excellent," replied the voice. "You're on the right track. Keep up the good work."

Before Raj could get another word out, the ground disappeared from under him He plummeted, screaming at the utter shock of his instant freefall. The air whizzed by him as he gained speed towards an endless abyss. But then a sudden jolt caused him to keel over.

The freefall stopped, and Raj felt solid ground beneath him. He found himself sitting upright in a bed in another unfamiliar room. Bandages blotched with red stains adorned his arms, but his wrist top wasn't in its normal spot on his wrist. Raj searched the bedsheets and the bedside tables without any success. Without his wrist top to keep him company, Raj's mind went back to his dream.

"That dream again," he thought.

His dreams were never so real before the junkyard. The floor. The smell. That mysterious man, or whatever it was. He wanted to brush it off, but had this sinking feeling it wasn't just a dream.

A voice emanating from the corner of the room distracted him from his thoughts.

"You're up."

Raj looked over to see the last person he expected. The Major sat in a wooden chair with her arms and legs crossed. Raj stared hard to get her into focus. Her untethered hair flowing over her shoulders was long enough to touch the waist on her jeans. It was a night and day difference from when they'd last met.

"Where am I?" he muttered. "Where is my wrist top?"

Raj's senses returned, bringing the pain along with them. His head and arms throbbed with the rhythmic beat of his heart.

"In safe hands," she replied. "And your wrist top is fine. We are just examining it. The more important question is how you are feeling."

"My head and arms hurt, but other than that I'm fine," he assured.

Raj sat there with his face in his hands. Soon enough, the memories flowed back into his head. Robert, the ship, the explosion...

"Wait," he thought, "if it wasn't Robert that saved me, then where is he?"

Raj wondered if he had escaped before the ship went up in flames.

"I was actually kind of surprised you kept our appointment," The Major added, bringing Raj back to the present. "The name is Candice by the way. I'm not really a fan of being called The Major, but it's my code name."

Raj thought for a moment until he remembered why he was at the ship in the first place.

"We never got to have our meeting," he said with a smirk.

"You're right, we didn't. So let me show you now."

Candice stood up from her seat and motioned for Raj to do the same. Raj pushed himself out of the bed and got to his feet. His whole body felt weak, but he was able to move without serious pain. Candice then opened the door behind her, and Raj followed her through the opening into an illuminated hallway. The white walls held a series of doors within their flanks.

"As you already know, there may as well be no rules in the lower zones," said Candice as they walked down the corridor. "The government does not supervise or protect us. They only care that we meet the demand of the products we make for them. We all do what we need to survive, but sometimes people do it immorally. That's where we come in."

They came upon a double door at the end of the hallway. Candice pushed the bar to open it, and Raj's eyes widened at what he saw on the other side. The door opened up to an enormous hall with a high ceiling. Raj and Candice stepped onto a balcony overlooking the network of people working in symphony.

"We call ourselves The Order," she said with a grin. "Like our name suggests, we are a group with the sole purpose of keeping order in the lower zones. God knows the lower zones need it."

"This is amazing!" said Raj.

They were about the only words Raj could think to say, but they made Candice smile from ear to ear.

"It's definitely come a long way, but we still have a long way to go."

Candice took one last look over the balcony before walking towards the stairway to their right.

"C'mon," she called, "there are some people you need to meet."

He followed Candice down the stairway and entered the organized chaos. People weaved through the catacombs of others clicking away at their keyboards. Others escorted people in handcuffs, presumably to a holding cell. Raj wanted to stay and watch, but stuck close to Candice as she weaved through the crowd.

They reached a door with the words "Do Not Enter" stenciled on the translucent glass. She twisted the handle and pushed through the passageway. On the other side was a tidy office space. A large bookcase with ornate legs lined the left wall, and a dark wooden desk on the far side of the room held various supplies. Raj followed Candice into the room and closed the door, muffling the noise coming from the large hall.

Raj's eyes caught some movement, drawing him to the space behind the desk. An elaborate grandfather clock stood on the far wall. It towered over the desk as if reminding the occupant of its importance. The rhythmic clicking of its inner workings echoed off the walls, assuring anyone who would listen that time continued its constant march forward. Intrigued, Raj moved in for a closer look. He traversed the room and stood face to face with the wooden spire. It was a thing of beauty. Skillfully painted Roman numerals adorned the face, and a display signifying the seasons showed a gorgeous cherry tree in full pinkish white bloom. Raj reached out his hand to touch the exposed face.

"I wouldn't touch that if I were you," said a voice from the far end of the room.

The familiarity of the voice caused Raj to swivel his head towards the origin of the sound. It was the guy Raj had hit in the face, along with the others there that day. He shook his head at Raj, looking at him with disgust.

"Rook doesn't like it when you touch his stuff," he said.

"Oh don't mind him!" one of them shouted.

"Yea," added another, "he's still a little upset about the shiner you gave him last month."

They all snickered at the remark, and Candice motioned for Raj to join the group.

"C'mon, I'd like you to meet the team."

Raj walked over and stood next to Candice.

"Raj, I'd like you to meet Bear, Willow, Jax, and of course, Kingsley."

Bear, the man closest to him, beamed widely.

"Nice to meet ya!" he exclaimed, extending his hand out to Raj.

His gray stubble beard and sculpted face sat on what appeared to be a rigid frame of raw muscle. Raj shook his hand, almost wincing at Bear's vice-like grip. Willow was leaned up against the wall next to Bear, and simply nodded at Raj. Her dark lipstick, long-tailed coat, and her curly jet-black hair only added to her mystique. Jax and Kingsley sat across from each other. They just started a card game, each throwing down and picking up cards in rapid succession. They glanced over to say a simple hello and went back to their game. Jax was a dark-skinned fellow with a thick pointed beard. He looked like a nice guy, but Raj knew from their previous encounter he wasn't someone to mess with. Kingsley hadn't changed from when they last met, but he did look a little angrier with Raj in his presence.

"Well, that's the crew," finished Candice. "Now where is Rook?"

"Over here where you left me!" boomed a voice from the opposite end of the room.

Raj looked over in disbelief to see a man lounging in the chair right in front of the grandfather clock. With a big yawn he stretched his arms above his head and lifted his feet off the desk.

"Just taking a bit of a nap before you guys showed up."

Rook stood up from his chair and continued to stretch widely before walking over to the group. He removed the aviator glasses from his face, wiped his eyes, and turned to examine Raj.

"Now who do we have here?" he asked.

"This is Raj, the person I was telling you about," said Candice

Rook planted his hand on Raj's shoulder. He was taller than Raj, but shared his dark complexion. His lips cracked a slight grin amid the graying stubble covering his chin.

"I've heard a lot about you."

"You...you have?" Raj asked with amazement.

"Indeed I have," Rook replied. "I hope you become a fine recruit for The Order."

Rook pulled a dark brown cigar from his shirt pocket. The flick of his lighter and a few short puffs brought the cigar to life.

"Now, if you'll excuse me, I have to brief the rest of the team for their next assignment. We will sit down for a conversation soon."

Rook propped the cigar in his mouth and extended a hand to Raj.

"It was a pleasure talking with you," he said.

Raj shook his hand and nodded in agreement, but remained at a loss for words. Why would they choose him? Even from his quick glimpse of the rest of their skills, he knew he couldn't match up.

"Well, the cat is out of the bag," said Candice, interrupting Raj's thoughts. "C'mon, let's get some fresh air and leave these guys to talk."

She motioned to Raj to follow, and they both left the room. They went back up the stairs and into the white hallway. Candice opened a stairwell door, prompting Raj to follow. They climbed the narrow switchbacks until there weren't any more left to climb. The door opened to a flat rooftop underneath a dimly lit sky. Raj took in a deep breath, filling his lungs with the cool outside air. He wasn't conscious for the majority of his time inside, but it felt great to breathe flowing air once more.

"So what do you think?" she asked.

Raj held his silence for a moment as he walked beside Candice towards the edge of the roof. It was all so sudden that he couldn't think. Still, one question lingered in his mind.

"Why me?" he asked.

"Really?" asked Candice, looking at him in disbelief. "You may not have much of an ability yet, but you're tough. That's what we need amongst our ranks. I mean, you were still standing after the Obama, and that was one hell of an explosion!"

Raj's mind returned to that night. Was Robert ok? Who was that guy in the ship with him? Why were they both there in the first place? So much left unanswered.

Candice saw the concerned look on Raj's face.

"You ok, Raj?" she asked.

"Yea," he replied, dismissing the thoughts to the back of his mind.

They made it to the edge of the roof, leaned against its railing, and looked at the breathtaking view. The lights of the buildings illuminated the skyline, and the streets below crawled with the evening rush of people flocking toward their destinations. It was weird for Raj to be looking down on it instead of being in it.

"How long was I out for?" Raj asked.

Candice shrugged.

"Only since last night. Still, I bet the people who care for you are worried."

"I don't have any, at least not that I know of," he said through a nervous grin. "The oldest memory I have is from about a year ago."

Raj peered over the edge as if gazing into the past.

"I woke up on a cold alley floor wearing only a white lab coat. I didn't know where I was or how I got there. The coat had a nametag though. Rajesh Vasishth. I doubt that was even my name, but it was the name I took."

Raj laughed to himself. He couldn't believe he was telling his life story to someone who was almost a complete stranger. It hurt him to even think about having friends and family out there who didn't know he was ok, but there was something about Candice that made him feel more open to talking about his past.

Candice saw the pain in his eyes and hugged him, and Raj didn't know what to do. No one ever showed him affection, yet Candice hugged him like they'd been friends for years.

"I'm sorry you had to experience that," she said. "But I hope you know you have a home here. We are a family, and a family always looks out for its own."

Raj looked at her and smiled. Tears welled up in his eyes at the thought of having a place where he belonged. Candice let go of her embrace and smiled back.

"So do you even know what your placement is?" she asked him.

Raj didn't have a clue what she meant by that.

"What is that?" he asked.

She laughed.

"Your zone placement of course! Here, I'll check for you."

Candice reached out and took Raj's right hand in hers. She then pulled a slim, rectangular device out of her pocket and waved it above the underside of his forearm. Confused, Candice waved it over her own forearm. This time it beeped as it crossed over a specific point. Flustered, she tried it on both of Raj's forearms this time. Still nothing. Her mouth just gaped open as if she couldn't process what had just happened.

"You.....You don't have a placement," she said.

She murmured this to herself a few times before it finally clicked. Raj could see the confusion building in her face, but he didn't know why.

"What's the big deal about placement?" asked Raj.

Candice looked over at him in disbelief.

"You really *don't* know?"

She took a deep breath before starting her explanation.

"Everyone is born in the upper zones. But they give you a test right after you're born. If you pass, they return you to your family in the upper zones. If you fail, they sterilize you and assign you fake parents already in the lower zones. Most who fail get placed in 3. Some in 4. But Zone 5 is out of use."

"But that doesn't make sense," replied Raj. "Why do they even have the stupid zone test anyways?"

Candice shook her head.

"They tell us it is for the survival of the city. That we are better suited to help out the HIVE by living here. For most people that is fine. They don't know what they are missing. But for those who have seen the upper zones, it is a spit in the face."

"Wait, so you've been to the upper zones?" asked Raj.

"No, but I've heard stories from Rook."

Candice looked off into the distance.

"They told us we were not good enough for the upper zones, but that our placement isn't permanent. If we work hard, we can get there one day too. Even have children of our own."

She laughed to herself as tears welled up in her eyes.

"But no one ever moves up," she continued. "They get safety. They get comfort. We have to struggle to make ends meet and fight off anyone who wants to take our money from us. And the worst part is we can't even leave the HIVE. It shouldn't be this way."

The tears rolling down Candice's face left Raj speechless. She was such a strong person, yet here she was opening herself up to him. He wasn't sure what to do, but his instincts took over as he threw his arm around her shoulder.

"And it doesn't have to be," he assured her. "Isn't that why The Order is here? To make a better life for us all?"

Candice wiped off a tear and smiled.

"We are. And that's why we want you to join us. You have the willpower to make anything you want a reality. I saw that from Day one, and what happened at the Obama reaffirmed it."

She turned to look at him.

"The choice is yours," she continued. "We will give you a few days to decide for yourself."

"There's no need," said Raj. "I'm in."

Candice cheered and hugged him again.

"I knew you would! You have the power to change everything. You could bring on some real change with your lack of zone placement."

Candice let go to the sound of her wrist top beeping. She turned off the alarm and cleared her throat.

"I need to get out of here, but I will see you soon," she said with a smile. "Welcome to The Order."

At that she walked off towards the access door and vanished out of sight. Raj couldn't help but be ecstatic. Things were starting to look up. He found a place where he felt at home, and he also learned a little bit more about his past.

"No zone placement, eh?" he thought.

Raj set his gaze into the distance and saw the tip of the Phoenix Tower pulsing brightly in the dark sky.

"Maybe I will get to see you."

CHAPTER 13: TROUBLE IN PARADISE

The city was in motion. The sidewalks held the flow of the monotonous crowd of people heading to their destinations. They crossed the streets in perfect right angles, only halting for the occasional bus speeding through the corridors of the city grid. A monorail glided along its track between the distant buildings.

In a quiet room high above the sprawl stood Marcella looking down on it all. Her vibrant strawberry blonde hair shined in the mid-morning sun coming through the full-sized windows of her office. She smiled to herself as she sipped her cup of tea in silence.

"Look at them all," she whispered. "Going on with their daily lives. Faithfully carrying out their duties."

Her smile returned to her face as she took another sip of her tea.

"They are perfect."

Just then, a ringing emanated from the desk behind her. She rolled her eyes before using her free hand to press the screen of her sleek wrist top. A full-sized projection of a man materialized in front of her desk.

"I see you're still enjoying your morning time," said the man.

He was an older man with wispy white hair growing from the sides of his otherwise bald head. Half-rim glasses rested on his nose, and he wore a charcoal suit with a cobalt tie.

"It is the most peaceful time of my day," Marcella replied.

Marcella savored her last sip of tea as it vanished like the silence moments before.

"So to what do I owe this unexpected meeting, President Silverstone?" she asked as she spun around to face him.

The President cracked a nervous grin.

"Looks like someone wants to get straight to the point. Just wanted to see how things were in the Great city of New Amsterdam."

"As great, if not better than Columbia."

"That's not the rumor," the President disagreed. "The cargo shipment to the commonwealth, and the incident at the shipyard would have me suspicious."

Marcella smiled as she placed the empty tea cup on her desk.

"All just a coincidence, Arthur," she assured him. "My team is still investigating, but they have concluded both instances were accidents. It's not all that hard to slip and fall into one of those train generators. Sadly that's all it takes to stop them in their tracks."

Marcella looked down at her wrist top and pressed at the screen before continuing.

"But still," she continued, "I have my security on elevated alert in the event we are wrong."

Arthur studied her for a moment before replying.

"Well as long as you're on top of it. But if you ask me, all the incidences are just too close for me to think them coincidental."

He cleared his throat before changing the subject.

"Now for the real reason I called you. You will attend the parade next month, correct?"

"Of course!" proclaimed Marcella. "Wouldn't miss it for the world."

Arthur smiled.

"Good. I am planning a post-parade meeting. We have some important matters to discuss with the other senators."

Arthur looked around before returning his gaze to Marcella.

"I think the situation with foreign affairs will be coming to a head soon. We must figure out a solution before it gets out of hand."

"Don't worry, it will all be taken care of when the time is right," replied Marcella.

She smiled at him with assurance, and Arthur returned her smile. But a beeping sound resonating from Arthur's wrist top took his attention away from Marcella.

"Time to go!" he exclaimed. "See you soon, Marcella."

The hologram faded back into thin air, and Marcella once again found herself alone in her office. She turned back towards the window still brandishing a smile.

"All will be taken care of when the time is right," she murmured. "All that's left to do is sit and wait."

"Well isn't that something?"

The distinctive scratching of flint and steel illuminated the darkness just long enough to light Robert's cigarette.

"Huh, I guess I'm out of fluid," he scoffed before closing his lighter and stowing it in his pocket.

Robert sat on the edge of a roof, dangling his feet above the dark alleyway below. The streets hummed their usual nighttime song. The voices and footsteps of the people passing by sang in harmony with the buzzing streetlamps lining the sidewalks. However, there was one sound which stood out from the usual tune. The steady pulse of club music emanated from the building across the street. The unwavering beat rang like a beacon, calling Robert to his first high-priority target.

Robert took another drag and checked the time. He had been studying the mark for two weeks. She was difficult to track, but Robert found a pattern in her movements. She frequented the club across the street every couple of days, usually staying for about an hour. There was only one night a week it wasn't VIP only, and that night happened to be tonight. With any luck, his target would already be on her way to the club tonight. The only thing Robert could do was wait.

"Should be here soon if she's coming tonight," he muttered to himself.

Robert took one final pull of his cigarette and climbed back onto the roof of the building. As his feet touched back onto solid ground, his wrist top sprang to life with a sharp ring. He pressed the answer button, silencing the annoying beep.

"Yea."

A deep voice boomed through his earpiece.

"Phoenix. This is Commander Aesculus. I hope you've made progress on your assignments."

"Ahh Commander! Thanks for checking up," he said sarcastically. "I really need—"

"What you really need is to cut your disrespectful bullshit when you're talking to your commanding officer."

"Hold on," retorted Robert, but the Commander continued without giving him a chance to speak.

"Some of these marks have sensitive information or materials. When you eliminate your targets, make sure to confiscate and destroy anything they have on their person. Understood?"

Robert sat up straight and raised his arm in a mock salute.

"Sir, yes sir!"

Robert ended the transmission before Aesculus could reply, and went to go light another cigarette. He took a deep breath in frustration as his lighter sputtered its sparks without producing a single hint of flame.

"It's never a good thing when they want everything destroyed," he thought.

To Robert, it sounded like he was killing a rogue agent. In fact, Robert was almost sure of it. The mark was a Zone 3 transient, which gave her easy access to both Zones 2 and 3. She was good at hiding her trail, and she may have sensitive information. All the telltale signs of an agent of the HIVE.

Robert looked towards the large screen hanging above the club's entrance. The words "Club Paradise" flashed across its face, accompanied by bursts of colorful lights. Robert stared at the screen, transfixed by its glow. The lights reminded him of the old times before the war. A time when he was young and naïve. Before he knew the burden of the truth.

"Times were definitely simpler then," he thought.

A sharp beeping ended Robert's stroll down memory lane, signaling the time his target usually arrived.

"It's time."

Robert gazed over the edge of the building and scanned the streets. His eyes darted through the crowds like an owl searching for its next meal. Sure enough, Robert spotted his mark a block down from the club. As much as she tried to hide it, an experienced eye could see the subtle differences which made her stand out. She walked faster, had straighter posture, and unlike the rest of the inhabitants of Zone 3, she moved with purpose. Robert absorbed every possible detail as she approached; he looked for anything to help him identify her in the crowded club. Her clothes and multi-colored hair blended with the rest of the club goers, but her bright purple backpack made her an easy target.

"That's what I'm looking for. Now let's get this show on the road."

Robert walked over to the edge of the building and jumped onto the fire escape ladder. He rode it down to the floor and made his way out of the alley. As he peered into the street, he saw his mark enter the club. Everything was running smoothly, and Robert decided to proceed. He made his way across the street and into the club. Passing through the front doors brought him into a small corridor. A burly man in an undersized black shirt stood guard.

"Holding up the wall?" Robert asked as he pulled back his sleeve and revealed a bandage holding his chip.

He'd ended up removing the chip so he didn't have to worry about it, but held onto it for instances like this. Luckily for him, the bandage didn't rouse much suspicion. The bouncer scanned his chip without as much as a word and waved him on his way.

"So much for a warm welcome," Robert muttered to himself.

The music grew louder as he continued down the corridor, and soon he reached a set of doors. He took a deep breath and exhaled with a grin. Robert no longer cared for the jobs or the people he did them for, but he loved the thrill of the hunt. They were like puzzles to him, each unique in its own way. There were so many ways to put it together, but only one way was the best. It was Robert's job to find the best way.

"Let's get to work."

He pressed the releases on both doors and pushed them open in one fluid motion. The sound rushed over him like a wave crashing on a beach. Colorful lights whizzed and flashed over a sea of people moving to the beat. The air smelled of body odor, bootleg alcohol, and the occasional whiff of different vape flavors wafting through the air.

Robert forced his way through the mob and searched for his mark in the general vicinity. With little luck, he continued to scan as he pushed forward. The room's epicenter held an enormous elliptical bar lined with people waiting to order their poison of choice. As Robert peered down the bar, he caught a glimpse of the distinctive purple backpack hovering amongst the crowd.

"Jackpot."

Robert kept his distance as he watched his mark talk to the bartender. He began to empty his mind and let instinct take over. His muscles loosened, and his mind slowed. The deafening bass of the music became a distant buzz in the stillness of his head. All that mattered right now was the kill.

Robert slipped through the crowd and followed his mark as she left the bar. She made her way across the room and disappeared behind a door labeled "Employees Only." Robert fought through the crowd to catch up, made his way to the door and slipped in after her. The door closing behind him left Robert in the deafening silence of a well-lit hallway. Its plain white walls straddled a dusty tile floor. Robert looked around to gather a sense of direction. The hallway led two ways, and he could not see his mark down either. He studied the hallway to his right and noticed a path worn through the dust and dirt like footsteps through fresh snow. So Robert proceeded right, following the traffic.

Robert continued until the trail in the dust took a sharp right down another hallway. Robert pressed up against the wall and slowly inched towards the corner. He was about to look when a noise stopped him in his tracks. The sound of footsteps echoed through the otherwise silent hallways. Robert paused for a moment, listening to their strides.

"Two people. One much taller than the other. Not far away. Coming in this direction."

His choices were clear. Find cover and prepare to attack as they round the corner, or evade and let them slip by. He surveyed his surroundings and saw little cover besides the corner where he already stood. Even with that, the lack of protection from the hallway behind him meant someone could walk up behind him at any moment. He would be at a disadvantage if the encounter lasted more than a few moments, so Robert decided to hide.

He crept over to a nearby door and tested the handle. It turned in his hand, allowing him to slip inside. On the other side was a small, cluttered room. The single lightbulb hanging from a string illuminated the dusty sound and light equipment lining the walls. A small table in the center of the room held a clutter of papers, and Robert realized he'd just stumbled into a makeshift office.

The footsteps grew louder as the sinking feeling in Robert's stomach told him they were headed for this room. He looked around for a hiding spot and found an empty nook under a table in the corner of the room. The equipment piled next to it gave him plenty of cover to work with, and the lack of equipment at the table's end gave him easy access. With few other choices, Robert slipped into the nook and backed into the shadows.

The footsteps stopped outside as the door swung upon its hinges. Two bodies poured in and closed the door behind them with haste. They remained silent until Robert felt a familiar wave of energy pulse through the room. They were using a sound-canceling device invented before the war. Whether he wanted to or not, Robert was about to listen in on a private conversation. He just hoped they would cut it short. He still needed to find his mark before she left the building.

The two women started to argue almost immediately after the barrier went up.

"I thought we discussed this!" one of them yelled. "You can't be coming here like this. Even you will leave a trail!"

"I know, I know," replied the other. "But I needed to come now. We don't have much time."

"What happened now?" asked the first voice.

"I've caught wind of the agency doing some internal research. I needed to get you this before they get to me."

Robert heard the squeal of a zipper followed by some rummaging through a bag. After a moment of silence, he heard a gasp.

"Is that what I think it is!?" the first voice asked.

"Yes," said the other. "This is the key to everything. The first step to achieving our goals."

Robert heard the bag zip closed before it dropped down on the floor next to the opening. Now propped against the table's leg was the all-too-familiar purple backpack.

"Well, today's my lucky day," Robert thought.

The conversation continued, but to Robert it mattered not. Completing the objective was his only concern. The noise-canceling device was an exceptional touch. Now his silencer was only there to save his ears from minutes of incessant ringing. Robert took a deep breath and pulled the pistol from his coat.

"There's no clear shot from here," he thought. *"Looks like I'll need to break cover."*

Robert crept out just as his mark reached down to grab her bag. Time appeared to stand still as they locked eyes. Neither of them expected to be face to face beside the table, but unlike his mark, Robert didn't hesitate. He pulled twice on the trigger, sending two bullets into his mark's stomach. The other woman screamed and headed for the exit. Robert pushed himself fully out of cover and dropped her before she could reach the door. Satisfied the runaway was taken care of, he turned his attention back to his objective. His mark managed to prop herself up against some equipment. She coughed as she tried to stem the flow of blood leaving her abdomen.

"Your efforts are pointless," she said as she spat some blood out of her mouth. "Even if you do succeed, they're just going to kill you anyway."

Robert stepped up to her and pointed his pistol.

"I'd like to see them try."

He pulled the trigger once more, completing his objective.

Robert walked over to the table and picked up a device with a small screen and keyboard.

"This must be the device they were talking about, and the one Aesculus wants me to destroy."

Robert studied it for a moment.

"Well if they're set on parting ways with it, I'll just take it myself. But I'll need to do something for the rest of this."

He stowed it in his pocket and began to crumple all the papers on the table into a large mass. Once he gathered them all, he held the papers in one hand and pulled out his lighter.

"C'mon lighter, you got one more light."

Robert flicked the lighter until the tiniest flame rose from the wick. He pressed it to the edge of the paper and waited until the fire caught hold. Robert then pulled a cigarette from his pocket, lit it with the paper, and put the paper ball underneath some equipment before grabbing the noise canceler and leaving the room. He made his way back to the entrance and walked onto the street to the sound of the fire alarm. Robert took one last look at the building and disappeared into the night.

CHAPTER 14: TALES OF GHOSTS

"Again!"

The old, moldy curtains hanging above the stage waved as Raj's vision spun in and out of focus. Everything hurt. Muscles, bones, ego. They all throbbed as his sweat-soaked skin kept him stuck to the hardwood floor. Willow's voice echoed through the auditorium.

"It doesn't take all day to scrape yourself off the floor, so get up!"

Despite the still-spinning room, Raj managed to work himself to his feet. He steadied himself and once again got into a fighting stance.

After four weeks of intense endurance and strength training, Candice had decided it was a good time to have his first sparring session. However, it wasn't against her like Raj thought. Candice was tough, but Willow was tougher. She hit hard, moved fast, and had the stamina to back it up. If

Raj hadn't known better, he would have thought she was a machine.

"Good," she said as he squared up again. "Now this time do it like you mean it!"

Raj huffed with anger. She was supposed to be teaching him, not beating him to a pulp. He knew anger wouldn't help him, so he tried to calm himself down as they stepped into their circular dance. Raj threw his first punch, and Willow effortlessly dodged. She then grabbed the wrist of his extended arm and yanked Raj past her. He jolted forward, barely catching himself from another fall. He turned around to find Willow already on top of him. Raj dodged the first couple of punches before getting a swing in. She evaded and countered in one fell swoop, ducking down and sweeping her leg into Raj's ankles. Once again Raj found himself staring at the ceiling.

She stepped over him, gazing down on his disheveled body.

"You can't fight for your life."

Raj looked away with humiliation.

"Was I expected to put up more of a fight than that?" he thought.

"But," she continued, "You can take one hell of a beating."

She outstretched her arm, motioning for Raj to take her hand. He grabbed it and nearly fell over again as she pulled him to his feet.

"It doesn't matter how well you can throw a punch. If you can't take a punch, then you're useless."

Raj cracked a bloody smile. He was about to answer when a voice came from the corner of the auditorium.

"I see you've been hard at work."

Raj looked hard through the lights shining in his face to see Rook lounging in the seats.

"Take a break, Willow, you've earned it," Rook said as he motioned for Raj to come over.

Willow exited stage right as Raj hopped down to sit next to Rook. He was leaned back in his seat with his hands resting atop his stomach as if the small curve of his belly was specifically designed for that purpose. He adjusted his position and cleared his throat before addressing Raj.

"So, how do you like it?" he asked.

"It's great," replied Raj. "It feels good to have a family."

Rook grinned, patting his belly in satisfaction.

"It does indeed. A family looks out for each other. Doesn't matter if it's feast or famine. Your true family will always be there."

Rook positioned himself upright.

"Got something for ya."

He reached into his coat pocket and pulled out Raj's wrist top.

"My wrist top!" cried Raj. "I almost completely forgot about it with all this training I'm doing."

Rook held it out and gave it to Raj. He thanked Rook and put it back on his wrist. Raj couldn't believe he'd gotten it back.

"I could see you weren't treated the best before you got here," said Rook, taking notice of Raj's reaction. "You don't have to worry about that here. I just needed to make sure it was safe. We've never seen one of those models before."

Rook reached into his pocket again and pulled out an already cut cigar. He stuck one end in his mouth, and with the click of a torch, he lit the other end until it held a fiery glow. Rook puffed the cigar, creating rolling clouds of sweet-scented smoke.

"It also brings me to my next concern," he continued. "I want to talk to you about the night of the Obama."

"What about it?" Raj asked nervously.

"I want to know if you saw anything suspicious. Maybe some people or things that looked out of place. Besides the boat, of course."

Raj's heart sank. Should he tell him about Robert? Did he already know? Maybe this was a test. But he didn't want to give Robert up completely. He didn't even know if Robert made it out. Though there was that other guy in there too.

"I noticed a strange man walking around right before the accident," said Raj. "There wasn't really much I could tell about him because he disappeared pretty quickly. Next thing I knew, there was smoke coming from the ship. It blew up not long after."

Rook took another puff of his cigar and reclined in his chair again.

"What do you know about Ghosts?" he asked.

"Ghosts?" asked Raj. "You mean like the spooky, fly through walls kind of ghosts?

Rook laughed.

"No, of course not. Ghosts are elusive spies, skilled assassins, and battle-hardened soldiers. They act as one of the many shadow hands of the HIVE government. When the government needs something done with absolute discretion, they call in the Ghosts. The Ghosts have been known to work by themselves, or even in small units."

Rook puffed his cigar again, letting the clouds roll from his mouth.

"The reason I bring this up is that I believe the incident on the Obama could be a cover-up by the HIVE."

"But why would they blow up their own ship?" Raj asked.

"That's exactly what we're trying to figure out," Rook replied.

"You know what was on that vessel? Twelve stealth jets, and thirty-six ballistic missiles with a state-of-the-art guidance system. They are so accurate, they could hit a target the size of a penny from miles away."

Rook took another puff of his cigar and continued.

"There is only one other possible scenario, and that would be—"

Rook's wrist top beeped, distracting him from the conversation. He looked at the screen and pressed a button to silence the alarm.

"Hate to break this up, but I gotta get going," said Rook as he stood up. "If you ever find yourself in need of someone to talk to, I'm all ears."

Raj shook Rook's hand before he departed from the auditorium. But instead of following him out the door, Raj just sat there in the sound of his own thoughts.

"Why did Rook ask me about Ghosts? How does Rook know what was on the Obama? Does he suspect Robert attacked the ship? Is Robert even alive? Maybe Robert is a top secret operative for The Order. That would explain why I ran into Candice near Robert's hideout... But if Rook asked me about what happened that night, that would mean..."

Minutes passed as all the questions and possibilities whizzed around Raj's head. He needed to go someplace to clear his mind, and he knew just the spot. Raj went out the back entrance of the auditorium and down the hall. He made his way to a stairwell and climbed until he reached the roof. The cool breeze greeted him as he opened the door and headed towards the roof's edge. The view had a vantage point of the whole city, but Raj looked towards the dark abyss of Zone 5. The view of the buildings barely outlined in the darkness sent chills down his spine.

"To think this used to be a bustling area," he said to himself. "Now it's only trappers and scrappers who roam those streets."

"Gotta make a living somehow, right kid?"

Raj nearly jumped out of his own skin as he spun around to find the source of the voice.

"Who's there!?" he yelled, keeping his head on a swivel.

He heard a chuckle come from above.

"It's only me."

With that, Raj heard the familiar click and scraping of flint. He looked up to see Robert sitting on the ledge of the upper deck with his feet dangling over the edge. His face glowed behind the flame as he lit his cigarette.

"Robert!" cried Raj. "You made it! Oh, I can't believe it, man. You had me worried."

Robert closed the lighter, sending the rooftop back into darkness.

"That was nothing, kid. I told ya it was light work."

Raj was so ecstatic to see him alive, he couldn't even speak. There was a moment of silence before Robert spoke again.

"So I see I've been replaced. You got someone else to teach you to survive out here."

"Oh no, it's not like that!"

He didn't want Robert to get the wrong idea, but Robert just laughed at Raj's reaction.

"I'm just busting your balls, kid! They are a good bunch to learn from, and they will train you well."

"Wait, so you know them?" Raj asked. "Are you a member?"

Robert took another drag of his cigarette.

"Let's just say I used to roll with them in the past," he replied. "I was in the area, and figured I would drop by to see some old friends."

"I knew it," Raj thought. "*Robert is connected with The Order. But why isn't he with them now?*"

"You should join up again!" exclaimed Raj. "We are trying to fight for what's right and take the city back for ourselves. It's a cause anyone can stand behind."

Robert took another drag from his cigarette before flicking it into the abyss below.

"If you'd seen what I've seen, you'd realize there's no point in trying."

Raj turned away to look back at the view below.

"*How could he possibly believe that? There's always a reason to at least try,*" he thought.

Raj feared that he too might come to the same conclusion as Robert. Maybe there was no point. But the thought was put on the back burner as his mind switched to something more pertinent.

"Hey, what do you know about Ghosts?...Robert?"

Silence.

Raj looked towards the ledge to find it once again occupied by dark emptiness. Before Raj could say another word, he heard a different voice call out from behind.

"Thought I might find you up here. Mind if I join?"

Raj turned around to see Candice under the glow of the pale-yellow light. Surprised by her sudden appearance, he barely managed to get out a response.

"Oh no, not at all."

Candice walked up next to him and looked out into the distance.

"It's breathtaking, isn't it?"

172

Her damp hair radiated the fresh fragrances of her shampoo, nearly distracting Raj from the conversation.

"It looks eerie to me," Raj replied. "Imagine how many people used to live there, and now it's nothing."

Candice shrugged, continuing to peer out over the expansive void.

"I imagine that's how the outside looks without the city lights. It's the closest thing we'll get to being on the other side of that wall."

Raj thought about it for a moment. He knew it was possible to live outside the walls, but Robert had never gone into detail about what it was like.

"Do you really think it's all just buildings out there?" he asked.

"I don't know," replied Candice. "But I do know there is a place in Zone 5 that's so quiet, you can hear what's going on outside the wall."

"Really!?" asked Raj in amazement.

Candice grinned.

"Yup. Can't quite figure out what it is yet. Just sounds like a big whooshing sound. We can go check it out now if you want."

Raj felt his face grow hot as he looked her in the eyes.

"Sure," he said, barely managing to form any kind of sentence without turning it into a jumbled mess.

She smiled as she took his hand and pulled him away. Raj looked back to the place where Robert had been sitting moments before. Raj hadn't seen, or even heard Robert leave. He was annoyed, yet intrigued by it. It was a jerk move to leave without saying goodbye, and he'd done it without Raj even noticing. It was as if he was....

"Nahhh!" Raj thought. "If he was the Ghost, then who was that other guy?"

Raj turned his full attention back in front of him and disappeared down the dark stairwell.

CHAPTER 15: FINDING HOPE

"What is this place?"

Raj followed Candice from The Order's headquarters down towards Zone 5, but past the place where Raj normally entered. Before Raj knew it, he was standing on a platform propped above the crumbling city streets.

"This is a train platform," Candice replied.

She gave him a playful nudge and leaned in close to his ear.

"A word of advice. Don't touch the middle rail."

With that, Candice walked to the edge of the platform and jumped down. Raj trotted after her and looked down to see her walking along one of the rails. Raj let himself down onto the tracks and hustled to catch up. By the time he caught up, they were out of the station and into the open world.

"Where are we going?" Raj asked as he struggled to maintain his balance on the rail.

"You'll see!"

Raj thought about pressing her for a more concrete answer, but figured he wouldn't get much out of her. He came to realize that she liked surprises.

He continued to follow her until they found their path blocked by a long subway train. The door was emblazoned with a faded orange circle set behind a white letter 'D'. Candice looked at Raj with excitement, but soon realized he had no clue what he was looking at. Candice just giggled and shook her head.

"This is a train."

"What's so funny?" he asked.

Candice shrugged.

"I don't know, it's just the way you look at everything with such amazement."

"Well you would too if you were seeing this thing for the first time!"

He wasn't sure whether his current sass came from within, or from the fact he was balancing two stories above the city streets. At any rate, Candice seemed to like it.

"It's not my fault you're still a wittle baby," she taunted as she slid open the train's door.

Candice climbed into the car, and Raj followed right behind her. Seats and handrails lined the inside of the hollow car, and faded advertisements plastered the walls. The advertisements waited in their cases for the next set of prying eyes to see their top-of-the-line automobile, high-tech gadget, or masterfully crafted diamond ring. But the dust coating every surface was evidence enough that their messages would no longer be heard. Like those they would have appealed to, their products had long faded into the depths of time.

Raj took it all in as he stepped down the aisle.

"So these trains used to carry people places?" he asked.

Candice nodded.

"These did. But trains could pretty much carry anything."

"Wow," whispered Raj. "The HIVE must have been a lively place back in the day."

"It was. Rook told me that even before the HIVE was built, millions of people rode in trains like these every day."

Raj couldn't imagine millions of people living in Zone 5.

"So Zone 5 was the city before the war?" he asked.

Candice shook her head.

"Zone 5 is only part of the city which once stood here. The rest is gone."

After passing through multiple cars, they finally made their way to the front. Candice wrenched open the final door to reveal a small cockpit with dirty windows. Candice plopped down into the driver's seat and reached down beneath the center console with both arms. Raj began to put the pieces together and looked at her in disbelief.

"You're not going to try to drive this thing, are you?"

"Not try," she replied without looking. "Just need to reconnect the main relay."

"Does it even work?" he asked.

Candice laughed

"Why do you think it's sitting so far down the track?" she asked. "Needed to hide it somehow."

Candice continued to tinker underneath the console until Raj heard a loud click. The lights on the dashboard sprang to life, and a whirring sound emanating from within the train grew faster and louder. Raj peered down the aisle as all the lights flickered on one after another in a domino effect display. Just then, a voice came over the intercom.

"BING BONG. You have now departed 161st Street, Yankee Stadium Station heading south. Next Stop 155th Street."

Candice smiled at the look on Raj's face.

"Isn't it awesome? It would take us hours to get to the spot on foot. With this we'll get there in no time!"

Raj stood there in amazement.

"How, how did you find this?" he asked.

"Who else?" she answered. "There's a reason Rook is our leader. He knows the most out of all of us."

Candice adjusted the driver's seat and continued talking.

"We found it deep in Zone 5 a couple years ago and rode it back here. Had to clear the track in a couple of spots, but we've been using it for recon missions deep in Zone 5 ever since."

Candice gave the instrument cluster one last look before releasing the brakes and pushing on the accelerator.

"Hold onto something."

The train jolted as the locomotive pulled the slack from between the cars. Raj stumbled from the unexpected motion, but quickly regained his footing. The feeling was weird, but it was a good weird. The feeling of going so much faster than one's legs could carry them. Chills reverberated through his whole body as the train descended into a tunnel and carried them into darkness. Candice flipped the automated controls onto express mode and stood up from the driver's seat.

"Let's go sit down," she suggested. "We have a decent ride ahead of us."

They stepped out of the cab and found seats under the glow of the fluorescent lights. As they sat in silence, Raj realized he really didn't know anything about Candice.

"So if you don't mind me asking, what's your story?"

Candice tilted her head and shrugged her shoulders.

"Same as anyone I guess. Left school at twelve years old and was forced to fend for myself. Got caught pick-pocketing a man. Luckily for me, that man was Rook. He took me in, and I've been with him ever since."

"Wow, so Rook's been with you through pretty much everything," replied Raj.

Candice smiled.

"Yup. He trained and raised me, making me wise to how the HIVE works. Sort of like I'm doing with you."

Raj returned her smile, but watched as hers faded.

"I will miss it when you know everything there is to know," she continued. "When I have nothing left to teach you, we won't hang out as much."

"What? No!" Raj disagreed. "You are showing me all this awesome stuff, and I really appreciate it. It doesn't matter what we do. You are just an awesome person to be around, and I would never stop hanging out with you."

Raj put his hand on her back, and she nestled her head into his shoulder. He held her in silence for a moment, catching whiffs of the sweet smells wafting from her hair. An overall sense of contentment rushed over him. The sound of the tracks clicking beneath him, the warm feeling of Candice in his arm. It was one of those feelings he wished he could keep bottled up for those days he needed them most. Everything in the world just felt right.

But the world had other plans.

The train lurched forward under the sound of the metal wheels grinding against the rail. Raj flew out of his seat, but Candice scooped one arm around his waist to keep him from tumbling to the floor

"What's going on?" Raj asked.

"I don't know," Candice yelled back. "We shouldn't be there for another twenty minutes."

Candice pushed Raj back into the seat and stumbled towards the conductor's cabin. Inside, the instrument cluster flashed and beeped its warnings.

"Obstruction on the track. One hundred meters," warned the computer.

Candice scrambled back out of the cabin and grabbed Raj on the way.

"We have to move!" she commanded, dragging him by his shirt towards the back of the train.

Although the train had already slowed considerably, Candice did not want to take any chances. They made it to the second car just in time for the train to make contact. All the cars jolted and hopped as they pushed together like an accordion. Candice and Raj tumbled to the ground as darkness and silence filled the car.

Candice groaned as she lifted herself from the floor. "You ok?" she asked.

"Yea, I'm good," Raj replied. "Where are we?"

Candice helped Raj to his feet and brushed herself off.

"That's what we're going to find out."

She pulled out her flashlight and led Raj back towards the conductor's cabin. Candice popped into the conductor's cabin to see nothing but darkness. She smacked the dashboard a few times and brought it back to life.

"We are lucky the autopilot saved us," she said as she assessed the dashboard. "But the train's computer will need some time to reboot before we can get out of here."

She reached into the cabin and flipped a toggle switch, causing all the doors to slide open. As Raj followed Candice down the aisle, they were met with nothing but wall surrounding them. But they saw a little light as they approached the back of the train. Out of the very last door, a single fixture illuminated the platform outside. The old tile still reflected the light, making it easier to see.

"Well, at least we made a station," said Candice with relief.

They stepped onto the platform and made their way up a set of stairs. Their footsteps echoed as they climbed ever higher towards the outside world. Soon they came up to a line of large metal barriers blocking their way. As if she was reading his mind, Candice spoke before Raj could even ask what they were.

"They called these turnstiles. They were essentially used to ensure people paid for the train."

Candice found one opening and pulled Raj along with her. The rotating arms clicked as he passed through, noting the first human presence in decades. They continued along their route and up one more set of stairs. The smell of fresh air grew stronger as they ascended to the outside world. A faded purple sky outlined the buildings towering on their left, but on the other side of the street held a vast openness unlike anything Raj had ever seen before.

"What's over there?" he asked.

"I don't know. Rook never took me here before. We do have some time to explore though."

They crossed the street to get closer to the opening. There appeared to be a path in front of them which led deeper into the clearing. Candice approached the large plaque fastened to a rock at the beginning of the trail.

"Central Park," she murmured, reading through the dust.

Candice continued down the path, leaving Raj no choice but to follow. As they explored their surroundings, the flashlight revealed large, twisted stalks planted haphazardly across the area.

"I have never seen such a large space without buildings in it," remarked Candice. "Not to mention these things sticking out of the ground."

Raj laughed because he was thinking the same thing.

"I was hoping you would know what those were," he replied.

It wasn't long before the first signs of sunrise showed in the sky. The purple turned into a light hue of blue, allowing Raj and Candice to follow the path much more easily with the added light. They were surrounded by more of the grim stalks, but wispy green tufts poked out of the ground around them. The green tufts grew denser and taller, and soon the waist-tall shoots stretched as far as the eye could see. Raj ran his hand through the shoots as they walked, until something in the distance caught his eye.

"Look, over there!" he pointed out.

Candice peered in the direction he pointed and nodded.

"Yea, I see it too. Let's go see what it is!"

They continued to follow the path towards the object in question. The air grew thick with an earthy aroma, and the rising sun brought the object into better focus. It was large and wide, but nowhere near as tall as a skyscraper. It looked like a giant bushy mass sitting on top of one of those dead stalks they'd passed along the way. The walkway led right up to the strange object, allowing them to get up close and personal.

"Whoa," said Raj as he noted the object's sheer size.

Candice noticed the sign staked next to the tree, and once again read its contents.

"The Hope Tree," she whispered as she read it. "The very first tree planted in the HIVE was planted in 2043 by Entrepreneur Sebastian Phoenix. As a tree genetically engineered to withstand the challenges of HIVE living, he thought it to be a great symbol of hope for future generations. 'As long as this tree lives, there is still hope for the future of mankind.' The grass in the surrounding lawn is the first grass engineered for the HIVE."

As Candice read the passage, Raj gazed into the canopy of the tree. He had never seen something so intricate, with all the intertwining branches filled with leaves. It was simply magical. He looked down at the massive trunk as it grew lighter in the rising sun.

"So this is a tree," he whispered in awe.

He rushed over to Candice and lifted her up off the ground. She shrieked with playful excitement as Raj spun her.

"We found a tree! We found a tree!"

Their eyes met as Raj put her down on the ground, and they stared at each other for what seemed like an eternity. Raj placed his hands on the curves of her hips and kissed her under the rising sun. He pulled back as he felt his face turn a bright shade of red.

"I'm sorry," he said. "I don't know what came over me."

Without a single word, Candice jumped on Raj and kissed him back. Raj stumbled under the surprise attack, and they both fell into the tall grass.

Raj woke up a few hours later to a bright blue sky overhead. Candice's head and arm rested on Raj's bare chest as she continued to sleep. The scent of her hair mixed with the fresh smells coming from the grass, and the tree provided shade from the bright sun. He couldn't believe the paradise they'd found hidden in Zone 5, and he wished they could stay there forever. But Raj knew the tranquility wouldn't last for long. The alarm on Candice's wrist top beeped, and she stirred from her sleep to turn it off.

"Good morning," she said as she looked at Raj with a smile.

She placed her head back down on Raj's chest, and he kissed her on the forehead.

"Good morning, sleepy head. How were your dreams?"

"Amazing... I don't want to go back."

"But we have to," replied Raj. "We both have pretty busy schedules today."

Candice got on top of Raj and looked him in the eyes.

"Our schedules can wait another twenty minutes."

Raj looked back at her and couldn't help but grin from ear to ear.

"Yes, they can definitely wait."

CHAPTER 16: A SECRET KEPT

A slight breeze swept through the air high above Zone 2. The darkness of the night sky obscured most of the surrounding surfaces, but the lights lining the streets below gave Robert an idea of how high he'd climbed. His next objective sat only a few stories above him, and he continued at his steady upward pace. The objective was simple: kill the target, and introduce a file into the computer system. Getting to his objective proved to be a more difficult task. The front entrance remained guarded at all hours, and even if it hadn't been, Robert still couldn't get the specific company access codes for the building. Luckily for him, he had a few tricks up his sleeve.

"It's a good thing I got full use of Nelson's stash," he said to himself. "I woulda never imagined finding a pair of these bad boys in working condition."

The things Robert referred to were the boots and gloves helping him scale the building. They worked by forming a magnetic-like attraction to any surface, and were the same model Robert used in his days as a Ghost. But the thoughts of nostalgia were not enough to distract Robert from the task at hand. He climbed until he got to his destination and peered inside the window of the private office.

"Looks like no one is in there, but the computer is still on. Guess I'll start on part 'B' of the objective."

Robert pulled a laser cutter from his pocket, cut a circle in the glass, and pushed it into the office. It landed on the carpet with a loud thud, allowing Robert to slip inside. He stepped over to the computer, plugged in a disk drive Aesculus had given him, and began typing away at the keyboard.

"Just gotta enter the database here.... and the file is downloading."

Robert pulled the pistol from his coat and began to screw the silencer onto the end of the barrel.

"With that out of the way, I just gotta find—"

THUD!

Robert looked up at the noise and saw his target standing in the doorway. His belongings lay scattered on the floor, and he looked at Robert in terror.

"Easy now," said Robert as he tightened the silencer into place. "There's no need to panic. I'm just here to talk."

"You're lying!" the man replied. "I...I know who you are!"

Robert raised his pistol as the man began to sprint down the hallway. His pistol fired three times, but each shot missed its mark and hit the wall.

"Damnit, why do you have to make things difficult?" sighed Robert as he hopped over the desk in pursuit.

He exited the room to see the man rounding the corner at the end of the hall. It would be a waste of ammo to try and take him out from this distance, so Robert tore after him to close the gap. He rounded the corner to find his target nowhere in sight. The maze of cubicles before him remained silent, but Robert's gut feeling told him they weren't empty. He crept through the maze, searching each cubicle one by one. After a few minutes of fruitless searching, Robert thought his gut feeling may have been wrong. But the sound of a door clicking to a close drew his attention to the other side of the room.

"He's taking the stairwell," Robert said to himself as he looked at the bright red exit sign above the only door in the immediate area.

Robert tore through the cubicles to the door, pushed it open and listened. The sound of footsteps echoed through the stairwell above him, and Robert ascended the stairs to continue the chase. He climbed higher and higher, stopping every now and then to listen for the footsteps continuing upward through the stairwell. Soon Robert could hear the footsteps without needing to stop.

"I'm getting close," he thought. "He must be running out of steam."

Robert closed the gap step by step until the sound of a door bursting open echoed from above. After a few more flights, Robert found himself face to face with the door to the roof. He kicked it open without breaking stride, and sure enough, Robert found his mark keeled over and panting from exhaustion.

"You shouldn't have run," said Robert as he placed a cigarette in his mouth. "You only made it harder on yourself."

Robert stepped closer to the man, lit his cigarette, and pulled his pistol from its holster before continuing.

"If you know who I am, then you would know there was no point in running. One way or another, you are dying tonight. It's nothing personal, I'm just doing my job."

His mark continued to pant, but looked towards Robert and held his hands in the air.

"Wait!" he cried. "You don't have to kill me. I can help you, Robert."

The sound of his own name made Robert drop the cigarette from between his lips. He closed in on the man and pressed his pistol against the man's head.

"You can start by telling me how you know my name! Who are you?"

The man looked up at Robert with a sudden realization in his eyes.

"You don't know anything, do you?" he asked.

Robert pressed the pistol harder against the man's head.

"You're about to know nothing if you don't spill the beans!"

"Please don't kill me!" said the man as he cowered in fear. "I'll tell you everything I know about you and Operation Phoenix Rising!"

"Then start talking!"

The man took a deep breath and began to speak, but the sound of a gunshot rang through the air. He fell to the floor as the blood poured from the newly formed hole in his head. Robert spun around to look for the source of the bullet, and it wasn't long before he spotted the drone whizzing towards him from beyond the roof's edge.

"Calm down, Mr. Phoenix," boomed a voice emanating from the drone. "It's only me."

Robert recognized the voice, but still didn't holster his pistol.

"Commander Aesculus," he called towards the drone. "I must admit, you're shorter and more metallic in person than I would have thought."

"Quiet Phoenix! I didn't come here to play games."

"Then what other reason would make you come here and kill my target?"

"Looked more like an interrogation than an assassination if you ask me," replied Aesculus.

"Crap, how long was he there?" Robert thought. *"He couldn't have heard anything I said with the drone being that far away, but I still need to think of something fast."*

"We were just about to have a little wager," said Robert as he pulled an old half-dollar coin from his pocket.

"If it landed on heads, I'd blow his brains out. If it landed on tails, I'd kick his ass off the roof. But thanks to you, we'll never know how that woulda turned out."

Aesculus laughed.

"Sorry to ruin your fun, but I've got a surprise for you that might alleviate your boredom."

"Did you get me a pony?" asked Robert. "I've always wanted a pony."

"Not quite," Aesculus replied. "Pack your bags, you're going to Columbia. We'll have the mission details forwarded to you within the hour."

At that, the conversation ended and the drone disappeared into the night sky. Robert lit another cigarette and exhaled the smoke. Aesculus arriving out of nowhere seemed suspicious to him. He could have easily called him over the wrist top, but he'd piloted a drone to Robert's position and taken out his target before Robert could get any information. Robert wondered if Aesculus watched him every time to make sure slip-ups like this didn't happen.

"And what's the deal with this Operation Phoenix Rising?"

Robert took a deep drag and exhaled slowly. He knew something fishy was going on, but right now wasn't the time to worry about it. The best thing he could do was head home and prepare for his next mission.

CHAPTER 17: THE RUSSIAN COLLUSION

"Da, I'm ready."

The man hung up his cellphone and slipped it into the pocket of his charcoal suit. The city streets bustled with the daily grind. Bodies moved like clockwork, almost oblivious to the tall man standing in their midst. He looked around to double-check his bearings. A large stone spire towered high into the gray sky above him. It looked out of place in the middle of the manicured lawn, but it did make a perfect landmark. The man oriented himself with the spire behind him and joined the crowd of people heading down the street.

The walkways and intersections overflowed with people, their paths interrupted only by the occasional car or bus whirring through the street. It was an unusual sight for the man. The cities back home were less crowded; the people more mindful. Here they didn't stop to say hello or acknowledge anyone on the streets, they just went about their day. Their lack of social interaction didn't matter though. It merely served to help him complete his mission.

The yells in the distance told the man he was close, so he pushed forward through the crowd until his destination came into view. There at the other end of the manicured lawn sat a pristine, white building. His only obstacles were the wrought iron fence, and the distressed mob lining its perimeter. They waved their signs and yelled in protest at the failures of their government.

The man shook his head and kept moving. He couldn't risk getting tied up in their battles, the mission was far too important to fail. But the screech of tires sliding on the pavement caused him to stop in his tracks. An armored truck rounded a nearby corner and squealed to a halt in front of the protesters. Men in riot gear poured out of the back and formed rank as their leader climbed atop the truck's hood with a megaphone. He directed it towards the crowd and turned up the volume before delivering his warning.

"Citizens of Columbia. This is Captain James Hunt of the Columbia Special Security Task Force. You are in direct violation of multiple laws, including picketing, unlawful zone crossing, and expressing seditious speech. These crimes are punishable by personality modification and/or imprisonment. You have exactly two minutes to vacate the premises without consequences. If you don't, we have no other choice but to use force."

Some of the protesters filed out as the Captain's grace period began, but most of the crowd continued to belt out their deafening roar of chants. They waved their signs and threw trash at the armed guards, but Captain Hunt and his men stood their ground. After the allotted time passed, Captain Hunt jumped down from the hood and took his place in front of his men.

"Time to go!" he yelled, motioning them forward.

His men spread out into a line and fired their shock rifles. The roar of the crowd turned into screams as the volleys of electric bolts struck their targets. Those who weren't incapacitated or fighting pushed through whomever they could to escape the madness. Chaos flooded the streets, giving the man the perfect opportunity. He reached into the breast of his suit, pulled out his pistol, and shot the man sitting behind the wheel of the truck. The shot echoed through the buildings as the bullet pierced the glass and hit its target. When no one seemed to notice, he sprinted over and pulled his victim out of the truck before hopping in the driver's seat and putting the truck into drive.

It lurched forward and picked up speed as the man steered towards the crowd. Officers and protesters alike darted out of the way, leaving a clear path to the fence. The truck smashed through the fence and steamed across the lawn towards its target. Bullets ricocheted off the truck as the man steered towards the white building's door and stomped on the accelerator. The truck crashed through the doors and screeched to a halt amidst the debris. Unaffected, the man hopped out with his pistol in hand.

He brushed himself off and walked through the corridors he'd studied so well. From this point on he could do it blindfolded if he needed to. Closer and closer he got, taking out the agents standing in his way. Finally, he reached a grand set of double doors and kicked them open.

There were two men in suits whom he dispatched with ease, and a table full of surprised politicians. As expected, the man had caught his target mid-meeting. He looked straight down the table, making direct eye contact with the wispy-haired man sitting at the far end.

The man walked toward his target, brushing more debris off his suit as he did. He reached his destination and cracked a smile as he pointed his gun between the target's panic-stricken eyes. The target cowered in fear as the whole crowd gasped at the man's final words.

"My boss sends her regards."

BANG!

For a moment the world stood still. But the man wielding the gun dropped to the floor as a team of agents flooded in towards the unscathed target.

"Are you okay, Mr. President?" one asked as they cleared the room.

"Y-y-yes," he stammered. "Thanks to you guys I am."

2 Hours Later...

"Ok, give me the scoop on this guy."

The president sat at the head of a different table lined with the same advisors and governors.

"He's Russian or Eastern European by the sound of his accent," one of them claimed.

"Accents mean nothing. Who does he work for, and where does he come from?" the president asked.

"He's not talking, but we did manage to pull some information from his ID chip," replied another. "His first trace in the city was picked up coming off a bullet train from the north."

"Which could only mean one thing," the president interrupted. "He had to get through—"

"New Amsterdam," finished a female voice.

A hologram of a feminine figure walked up to the opposite end of the table from a dark corner of the room. Her fiery red hair streaked down to her tight shoulders. President Silverstone cleared his throat to address the rude interrupter.

"Senator Phoenix. Nice of you to join us. You were supposed to be here in person for today's meeting."

"But it's a good thing I wasn't," Marcella exclaimed. "Who knows what could have happened if I hadn't been called away for urgent business."

She didn't seem to notice Arthur's annoyance with her and continued.

"The urgent business pertained to tracking down this very individual. The man's ID comes back as Marcus Finch. A model Zone 2 citizen if you ask me. The only problem is the real Marcus died well over a decade ago."

"How did that get by you?" the president asked. "With the way your security is, you should have caught that on the spot."

"Well," replied Marcella, "I must admit that I'm quite embarrassed about all of this. But this fake was good. It seems his connection was able to pass him into New Amsterdam unnoticed and hack the AI's database. We're in the process of finding out who that connection is."

"Isn't it obvious?" retorted the president. "The Russians are behind this one. First the train incident, then the Obama, and now this. They have a mole within your ranks. Most likely there's more than one!"

He sat there in silence massaging his brow. His advisors whispered amongst each other before shouting in volleys.

"We must tighten security!"

"Yes, ban inter-HIVE travel!"

"Curfews for all residents!"

They continued to ring out ideas and argue amongst themselves while the president just sat there in silence. His body tensed up and his face contorted, but the frenzy was too great for anyone to notice. Finally, it became too much for him to bear.

"QUIIEETTT!" he bellowed.

The ticking clock echoed through the room as his startled advisors peered over in his direction.

"What we need to do next is obvious," said the president. "We must go to war."

"You forget that war at this point would be suicide," spoke Marcella from across the table. "Even if you do manage to unite every HIVE under this goal, our estimates project they still outnumber us."

"You forget that we left them broken beyond repair," President Silverstone argued.

"And YOU forget that they did the same to us; if not worse!" Marcella fired back. "That war ended decades ago, and we have been in near silence with them ever since. Who knows what they lost from the hacker Nostradamus, and who knows what they've been up to."

Arthur took a deep breath, exhaling it slowly.

"Then you should know what we need next," he replied. "You need to figure out that power source to save us all from the Russians. Your father must have backed up all of his work somewhere. And as for the prisoner, send him to Eisenstadt. I know crime and punishment is your gig. Perhaps you can get more information out of him."

Marcella cracked a cold smile at Arthur, looking him dead in the eye.

"It tends to do that. That is, of course, if it doesn't kill him first."

Marcella pressed a button on her wrist and found herself back in her cozy, top-floor office.

"How did that one turn out?" asked a deep voice from the corner of the room.

Marcella looked over to see a well-dressed man with dark skin and a bald head lounging on the couch across the room. He swirled the large cubes of ice around the confines of his rocks glass before taking a small sip.

Marcella sighed as she walked over to the bar.

"Not as well as that two hundred-year-old whiskey you're enjoying, Commander," she said.

She filled her own glass with ice and watched the whiskey crack the ice cubes as she poured it over them. Marcella then took a sip and savored the familiar warmth trickling down her throat.

"This has changed everything," she said before taking another sip. "We must hasten our timeline if we are to succeed."

Aesculus took a sip of his own drink before grinning at Marcella.

"Don't worry, Marcella," he assured her. "Robert has been going faster than expected. It seems not even old age can stop him."

"Good. We have another target to add to the list."

"Oh?" said Aesculus, intrigued by the news.

"Yes. We've found the missing asset from Project Blue Steel. It seems The Order has grown a liking for him and taken him in."

Aesculus took another sip from his glass.

"Do they know what he is capable of?" he asked with concern in his voice.

"I don't believe so," she replied. "I don't believe even he is aware of his own ability. At any rate, he must be taken care of. Can't have another Robert Phoenix roaming the city unchecked."

"That's for sure," agreed Aesculus. "That's for sure."

Chapter 18: Through Feast and Famine

A clear, monotonous blue sky hung over the ever-stirring city of New Amsterdam. Robert was high above the sprawl, absorbing it all in silence. The warm draft which climbed up the face of the building carried the faint sounds of the citizens going through their day. Despite knowing its false reality, it felt good to bask in the light of the glowing orb above him. It reminded him of the outside world, and how he yearned to return to it. Robert closed his eyes and kept them shut. He could almost picture himself on a rocky outcrop atop a mountain. His mind's eye sculpted the valley below. The trees created vast blankets of green, only halting for the river carving through the rolling mountains. The steady wind brought the smell of wildflowers and the sounds of Mother Nature at work. Robert took a deep breath and cracked a smile at the world he created. But the beeping of his wrist top pulled the plug, and Robert watched his wonderland swirl into nonexistence.

He opened his eyes to find himself back atop the building in the heart of Zone 3. Robert sighed as he turned off the alarm and reached into his pocket to grab his last cigarette. He lit it and savored the smoke filling his lungs.

This was the last job. Aesculus had told him so at their last briefing. After this, he would see if his sister would hold up her end of the bargain.

"*She better,*" he thought.

Robert kneeled down next to a high-caliber sniper rifle perched on the edge of the building. He nestled the butt into his shoulder and looked down the scope to survey the target area. The crowd gathered around a stage set for a speech. Robert watched his target walk onto the stage and take his place behind the podium. He shuddered as his target seemed to stare right at him.

"*You idiot,*" Robert thought. "*We made an agreement. We spent weeks making the perfect plan. Hours and hours figuring out every little perfect detail. Now you change the plan at the last minute and want to throw it all away?*"

Robert pulled his face back from the scope. It was all too real. He tried to think of any last-minute trick for them both to get out of this alive. But as much as he tried, he knew any deviation from the new plan would end in failure. He knew what he had to do.

Robert suppressed his emotions and brought himself back into focus. He chambered a round, re-sighted his target, and slowed his breath.

"Goodbye, old friend."

One hour earlier...

"All right team, gather around!"

Candice's voice traveled clear across the auditorium, bringing anyone who heard into a close circle. Raj couldn't believe it. It was the day of his first official assignment, and his stomach was filled with butterflies. He didn't know what to expect. Everything could go right, or everything could go wrong. But his current objective was listening to Candice, so he gathered around the circle and waited for Candice to continue.

"Ok guys, this should be a simple one," she said. "Yet, it still shouldn't be taken lightly. This is the first time in over four decades that our organization will come out of the shadows and make ourselves known to the masses. Before, we worked in secret. And now, we will show them who we are and what we stand for."

The whole group applauded and cheered, and Candice waited for it to die down before continuing.

"Initial reports from our teams already out there suggest a minimal risk from the crowd. Still, you all will be out there as undercover backup. You all know your positions, head to them now. We will start within the hour."

The group of about thirty quickly dispersed in their separate directions, but Candice stuck around.

"Delta Squad, hold back for a minute," she commanded.

Raj turned to leave, but Candice grabbed him and pulled him back.

"That includes you," she said.

Candice reached into her shirt pocket and handed him a patch. It was a black triangular patch with the scale of Justice in the middle of it. Around the edges were words from a language Raj had never seen before.

"You're officially one of us now; a part of Delta Squad," she said with a grin.

"Wait, are you serious?" asked Raj.

"Completely serious. You're still not a pro, but you've excelled faster than any recruit Rook has ever seen. He gave me the official orders to let you in today."

She gave Raj a quick, but tight hug.

"Welcome to Delta."

"Oooooh some squad romance going on over here!" said Jax as he joined the circle.

"You're just mad you can't get that close to me without getting your ass kicked," Candice fired back.

The rest of Delta Squad laughed as Jax tried to make up a comeback, but Candice quieted them down and continued with their meeting.

"Once again, I'm not expecting any issues, but I felt the need to inform you guys about some recent findings."

She handed out a manila folder to be studied and passed around.

"These pictures were taken a couple weeks ago, and are the only photos I could get of the Ghost. He left as quickly as he appeared, and I haven't been able to find him since."

"That can't be," murmured Bear.

His face filled with both confusion and disbelief as he stared at the contents of the folder.

"This is the same guy I saw as a kid. Musta been fifty years ago, but it looks like he hasn't aged a single day!"

Kingsley snickered.

"Wow Bear, you must be really old!"

"Shut your trap, Kingsley!" Bear retorted, slapping him across the side of his head.

They began to squabble with each other, but the look Candice shot them brought them back in line.

"I went against Rook's orders to find this guy, so this information is highly classified," she continued. "From this day forward, keep your eyes and ears peeled. If you catch any sort of wind about him, report it to me, and only me. Got it?"

The whole crew nodded in agreement, allowing Candice to get to her next point. Willow nudged Raj in the shoulder and passed him the manila folder. He opened it and froze, nearly spilling the folder's contents all over the floor. The first picture showed the outline of a man sitting on the edge of a building. The long hair and the sleek coat were quite distinctive, and the cigarette hanging from his mouth left Raj without a doubt.

"Robert...."

"You ok, Raj?"

He looked up to see Candice as the only one left there standing with him. The rest of the group was already on their way to their assigned positions.

"Yea..." he said, trying to stir the new discovery out of his head. "Just never thought I'd see the Ghost."

She smiled at him, doing her best to hide her own nervousness.

"Well let's hope you never have to. Now c'mon, we're going to make a quick stop before getting out there."

Raj followed Candice down a hallway leading deeper into The Order's headquarters. He tried to focus on the task at hand, but he couldn't wrap his head around the contents of the folder.

"How could he be the Ghost?" he thought.

Raj tried to find the answers in his head to disprove this theory, but the more he thought about it, the more it made sense. Robert could remain cool, confident, and collected with death breathing down his back. He could appear and disappear without a trace. Hell, he was even resourceful enough to get his hands on functional new and old-world technology. Raj had nearly forgotten that it was Robert who gave him the wrist top in the first place.

They reached the main hall to find it nearly empty. Instead of the hundreds of people going about their work, only a few people remained at their desks. Candice didn't seem to be bothered by this, and led Raj to Rook's office.

"What are we doing here?" Raj asked.

But Candice just opened the door and dragged Raj inside. She turned on the lights and walked towards Rook's desk.

"Don't you think this is the wrong time and place?" Raj asked as he looked around the empty office.

"Don't be stupid," replied Candice. "That's not what we're here for."

She approached the grandfather clock behind the desk and began to play around with the hands on its face. After a couple of seconds, a large click emanated from the clock, and it swung open to reveal a passageway.

"What the..." said Raj, but Candice just grabbed him and dragged him through the tiny hallway.

They came out on the other side in what appeared to be a lounge. The room was dark except for the lights hanging over the pool table on the side of the room. Raj followed Candice as she used a flashlight to guide them across the room and up a set of stairs. When they reached the top, Candice pointed to a door on their left.

"Go in there and wait for me," she said. "I need to check some last-minute things."

Raj nodded and slipped inside. The door opened into a cozy-looking foyer. The yellow walls stood as a warm background to the ornate furniture. Raj looked around the room only to find Rook lounging in a chair in the corner. He sat relaxed with his eyes closed, but must have realized Raj was staring at him because he opened his eyes to meet his gaze.

"Sit down, Raj," he said, unfazed by Raj's sudden appearance.

Raj took a seat next to him, and they sat in silence for what seemed like an eternity. Raj couldn't help but fidget around, causing Rook to break the silence.

"You would think you were the one giving the speech," he joked. "Anything bothering you?"

Raj forced a smile.

"It's a big day," he lied. "A day that will go down in history."

In reality his mind still struggled to wrap his head around Robert being the Ghost.

"You've got that right," agreed Rook. "It's just one speech of many more to come, but perhaps the last of mine."

A chill ran down Raj's spine at the sound of those words.

"What do you mean by that?" he asked.

Rook just smiled, staring off into the other side of the room.

"So, The Order's newest Delta Squad member," he said, changing the subject. "Have you ever thought about your future here, Raj? Any goals?"

Raj was taken aback by the switch in tempo. His future wasn't something he thought about often.

"Well no, not really. I'm just happy to be a part of something that makes sense. Something that could bring a positive change in our world."

Rook chuckled.

"You remind me of my younger self," he said as he continued to look off into the distance. "A young Corporal Nelson Figueroa."

He turned to Raj and rested his hand on Raj's shoulder.

"You will face many obstacles along this road. But one day you'll realize you will be a key player in making all that change possible. Just remember those who were there through feast and famine."

Raj was at a loss for words. How could Rook know such a thing with such conviction? It was as if he already knew what would happen. But just as Raj was about to speak, Candice appeared from the doorway.

"All right Raj, let's get going. Everything seems to be set."

"But," protested Raj.

He wanted to talk to Rook more, to figure out his words.

"Go on, Raj," said Rook. "I'll be right out after I have a few more minutes to myself."

Raj looked at him. He wanted to sit down with Rook and talk about everything, including Robert. But Candice looked at him with a sense of urgency.

"Raj, we gotta go," she said.

Raj lifted himself up out of the seat, said good luck to Rook, and headed back out the door with Candice. They crossed through a small store with empty shelves and went out the front door. They exited to the roar of the huge crowd

211

gathered for the speech. They all surrounded the stage in front of Lucky's convenience store, patiently waiting for Rook to make his appearance. Candice dragged Raj from behind the stage and pointed far down the street.

"Ok Raj, your patrol area is out there in the rear," she yelled into his ear. "Use your wrist top to communicate any suspicious activity. And remember to stay tuned for the scheduled check-ins. Otherwise, enjoy the speech. This moment could be the most pivotal in history!"

Candice snuck him a kiss before disappearing into the crowd.

Raj's mind spun out of control as all the information flew through his head, but he knew he had to keep his cool. He took a deep breath and took off towards his position in the back of the crowd. He slipped in and out of the openings between the people as he tried to get back there as fast as possible. The speech could start any minute, and he wanted to be ready. When he finally reached his spot, the crowd roared with excitement. Raj turned around to see Rook taking his place behind the podium. He waved to the crowd before motioning everyone to quiet down. But as the crowd died down, Raj noticed the lack of security stationed around the stage.

"Major, this is Falcon 2, do you copy?" he said into his mouthpiece.

"Copy Falcon 2, this is Major," replied Candice. "What is your situation?"

"All clear here, but I would like to point out there are no patrols on or near the stage."

The radio went silent for a second before Candice answered.

"Rook specifically requested he be left alone on the stage. We shall respect his wishes."

Raj disagreed with Rook's judgment, but confirmed the response on the radio. Why bother having security at all if he was up there alone? But all went silent as Rook began his speech.

"Ladies and Gentlemen," he said.

His voice boomed over the crowd, reverberating off the surrounding buildings.

"I welcome all on this wonderful day. Some of you may know me. But for those who don't, you shall very soon."

Raj scanned the crowd and saw nothing suspicious. All seemed to be intently listening to the speech. No weapons, no strange-looking people, and most of all, no Robert. That's who Raj was really looking for.

"For decades we have been mistreated and neglected, sometimes to the point where we can't even distinguish between what can and can't be changed. I remember a New Amsterdam with true freedom, and true pride for this city. We have fallen far since then, and have become the slaves of those living lavish lives in the upper zones. Well, I say that has to end."

Thousands of cheers echoed off the buildings in a deafening roar as Raj continued to scan for anything suspicious. He glanced down the empty street behind them, and was about to turn away when something in the distance caught his eye. A tiny glimmer of light reflected from the top of a building at the end of the street. It only lasted a second, but Raj continued to look.

"*What made that light?*" he thought. "*It wasn't a window.*"

The windows he could see did not reflect the sun no matter how he moved. But then the light flickered again, followed by a bright flash twice its size.

CRACK!

The loud, yet precise sound of a rifle cut through the air, sending the crowd into a panic. Screams echoed all around him as Raj turned around to see an empty stage. The white backdrop curtains glowed with spatters of red, and a few people jumped up on the stage and knelt around a spot behind the podium. Raj couldn't see Rook. His eyes darted around the stage until the reality of the situation dawned upon him.

"No..."

Raj sat frozen amidst the chaos until the anger boiling inside sprang him into action. He sprinted towards the building, weaving through the stampede of people now fleeing away from the stage. Just then, the headset in his ear sprang to life with chatter.

"Falcon 2, status report!"

Raj was going so fast, he couldn't tell who it was on the other side.

"Rooftop of the tan building, north side!" he yelled into the mic.

He reached the building in record time and tore his way up the stairs. The flights seemed endless, but he continued to climb them at full speed. His lungs were in pain and his body ached, but he knew he could not stop. The roof door came into view, and Raj nearly kicked it off the hinges as he breached the roof. He was prepared to fight anyone or anything up there. Yet except for a few boxes, the rooftop lay empty. Raj walked over to the edge and looked down upon the street below. He could see the stage clear as day from his current vantage point.

"How could we have not seen this?" he asked himself. "How could I have failed?"

Tears streamed down his face, but before he completely lost his composure, his nose caught onto a faint smell. A smell so familiar, yet so foreign, he couldn't quite put his finger on it. He looked around to find the origin of the smell, and it wasn't long before he found it. Raj bent down to the floor and picked up the speckled filter of a cigarette. It was warm to the touch, and the last of the tobacco still smoldered inside.

Suddenly the door behind him burst open, and Raj spun around to see Candice with her gun drawn. She did a quick scan of the rooftop before holstering her pistol.

"There is no one here. All clear," she said into her mic.

"But there was someone here," said Raj.

As he looked at the butt between his fingertips, there was only one word he could manage to force out.

"Robert."

Chapter 19: The Flight of the Phoenix

The city felt unusually quiet. Well, maybe not for Zone 5. The dark ruins of the buildings lay in near darkness, their deformed and tumbled corpses outlined by the faint light stretching from the upper zones. Despite the dilapidated appearance, Robert found solace in the stillness. Not a chirp, squeak, whisper, or howl. But if he listened closely, he could hear the waves crashing hard against the wall surrounding the city.

"It sounds like there's a storm outside," he said as he looked up at the starless void. "Yet no matter how hard it rains out there, it's always nice in here."

Robert had already relayed his success to Aesculus, and was awaiting a reply. He'd spent all week preparing to leave the HIVE. His necessities were packed, and his motorcycle was full of hydrogen. Robert had even mounted the compressor tank to the front fork to double its range. Although it would have been nice to have the solar panel too, Robert had a feeling he wouldn't be staying at the Phoenix Estate anymore. He wouldn't know for sure until he got the call from Aesculus.

As the minutes turned to hours, his mind couldn't help but wander to that fateful moment atop the roof. His finger still itched in the spot where it pressed the trigger, and his mind's eye replayed the bullet's flight over and over. Robert tried to push the thought from his head, but it wouldn't budge. The pain and anger built up in his body until it became unbearable. He was about to scream when his wrist top beeped from an incoming call.

"Hello," he said, picking up the call in one ring.

"Well, someone sounds like they're a bit tense," answered Marcella.

"I'm surprised to hear your voice instead of your little puppet," Robert fired back.

Marcella laughed.

"My 'little puppet' is off on a special mission. But he did relay to me the news of your success. Good job, Robert! You never fail to impress."

"Let's cut to the chase and get to what's really important here," said Robert, dismissing his sister's compliment.

Marcella paused in frustration.

"If you insist," she said, before clearing her throat to continue. "I have another job for you. You are —"

"Now wait a God damned minute!" shouted Robert. "Aesculus told me that job was my last. Are you going to honor our agreement, or not?"

Marcella chuckled.

"Oh, Robert," she said playfully before settling into a serious tone. "You forget that entering the HIVE and taking on this contract means that I OWN YOU! You're going to do this mission for me. Then, and only then, will I honor the terms of our contract. Now, be a good brother and look over the details of your next target."

Robert grimaced at her as he switched the screen on his wrist top to view the incoming data. What he saw sent chills down his spine. Although Marcella had redacted most of the file's information, the attached picture left Robert without a doubt. His final target was none other than Raj. Robert did his best to sound unassuming as he scrolled through the contents.

"What do you want with a kid?" he asked Marcella. "And don't feed me no bullshit. It's one thing to kill an old friend, it's another to kill someone barely old enough to grow a full beard."

The line went quiet for a moment, and although Robert could not see her, he felt her eyes bearing down upon him.

"Now listen here," she demanded. "The only thing you need to know is I want him dead. When he is, you will have your freedom. Is that clear?"

Robert remained silent as he looked over the dossier and soaked in what she said. He knew it was a long shot, but it was worth trying to buy as much time as he could.

"Give me five days," he said shortly. "That will give me ample time to determine his habits."

Marcella's demeanor changed within an instant.

"I knew I could count on you. I'll let you get to work."

She cut the transmission, and Robert wasted no time grabbing his belongings and descending the building. He had no intentions of killing Raj, but he also couldn't warn Raj of the hit without blowing his cover. The best thing Robert could do was leave the city as soon as possible.

Robert made it to the bottom, hopped onto his waiting motorcycle, and sped off towards Zone 2. He had everything he needed to make his escape, but he still had to figure out how to get out. If that book he found at the Phoenix Manor held any weight, the front gate would be the best way to leave. The current plan was to make his way to the gate, store the bike in the parking garage, and stake out the best time to slip by unnoticed. If all went well, he would have a couple days to put as much distance as possible between him and Marcella. He had no clue where he would go, but he knew the Phoenix Estate was no longer an option.

Robert dodged his way through the wreckage of Zone 5 until he crossed into the lit streets of Zone 3. With the cleaner streets, Robert was able to pick up the pace and make some time. Curfew was about to start soon, and he wanted to reach Zone 2 before it did. The automated guards on patrol ran a tight schedule, and there were few opportunities to avoid them. Luckily for Robert, the ride would be a straight shot.

The zone border came into view after twenty minutes of riding, and Robert looked down to check his wrist top.

"Just in time."

He didn't even get the chance to look back up before being smacked hard in the chest. Robert flew off of the seat and slammed to the floor as his motorcycle coasted pilotless down the street. He groaned as he lay on his back and tried to process what had happened. As his vision returned, he saw the rusty cable wobbling a few feet above his face.

"Who the hell strung that across the road?" he thought as he rolled onto his stomach.

A familiar voice spoke from the side of the street, but Robert was too disoriented to figure out who it was. When he lifted his gaze, he saw the last person he would ever expect. With pain surging through his body, and all the wind knocked out of his lungs, Robert could only muster up enough breath to get out one word.

"You."

"Yea, it's me. Are you surprised?"

Raj stepped over to Robert and lifted his arm to show off his wrist top.

"I bet you're regretting giving this to me right about now. You used its tracker to find me, but you didn't fully desynchronize our wrist tops when you gave it back. If you could track me, I figured there must be a way for me to track you. Sure enough, I found what I was looking for and used it to set the perfect trap."

"You've got a lot of nerve," said Robert as he struggled to get on his hands and knees.

"Well, you've got a lot to answer for," replied Raj. "You killed our best hope at freedom. And for what?"

"I don't know what you're talking about, kid."

"Oh, don't play coy with me, Robert," Raj fired back. "There are very few who can get a hold of firearms in the HIVE, and only one who has ever gotten cigarettes."

Raj pulled the old cigarette butt from his pocket and tossed it in front of Robert.

"Why did you do it?" he asked.

Robert chuckled to himself as he looked at the cigarette butt before him.

"I knew I shoulda saved that one for later," he said to himself, ignoring Raj's question.

Raj wound up and kicked Robert hard in the ribs. Robert coughed in pain, almost dropping from his hands and knees. Blood dripped in long strands as it mixed with the saliva Robert spat from his mouth. Raj pulled a pistol from his waistband and pointed it at Robert. But instead of getting a reaction, Robert looked down death's barrel unfazed.

"If you're gonna kill me, kid, just do it. You'd be doing me a favor, but it won't help you find peace."

"What would help me find peace is telling me why you did it!" Raj fired back.

Robert remained silent and averted his gaze back towards the floor. The anger surged through Raj's veins as he wound up for another kick. He threw his leg with all his might, but this time Robert mustered up enough strength to react. He pushed his body upright just in time to see Raj's leg sweep inches from his face. Raj tried to regain his balance from missing, but it was already too late. Robert gripped the gun with one hand and used his other hand to push Raj's leg farther towards the sky. Raj's planted foot came out from under him, and the pistol twisted away from his hand as he crashed down onto the floor. Now the tables were turned. Raj lay on the floor writhing in pain while Robert stood above him with Raj's gun in his hand.

"You just don't get it, do you?" asked Robert. "Do you think this is the first time someone tried to serve justice and restore order? Countless times this battle has been fought. Some lost their lives. Many have shed blood. All of them lost the fight. And even if they do succeed, all those who fought will die, and won't live long enough to see their heroic faction become the villain. All except me."

Robert seemed to zone off at those last words as if looking back at his memories. Raj knew Robert meant every bit of what he said, but Raj refused to believe him.

"It's worth the try," replied Raj. "It's worth the fight!"

Robert snapped back into reality and looked at Raj with soul-piercing eyes before cracking a little grin.

"I admire your valiance, kid, but I think it's about time you gave up. Your face has already landed itself on the HIVE's hit list."

Robert released the clip from the pistol, ejected the remaining round, and held out the pistol for Raj.

"They taught you well, but you still forgot the first rule I taught you. And you left the safety on."

Raj reached out for the pistol and returned it to his waist. Robert turned away without another word and limped towards his downed motorcycle, and Raj once again found himself speechless. Robert had just told him he was his next target. He'd had the perfect chance to end Raj's life, but he chose not to act on it. Robert may have been the Ghost, but he wasn't the heartless killer the legends played him out to be. A blood-frenzied killing machine wouldn't show humility like that. It was something Raj had known all along, but let the recent events allow him to forget.

"Where are you going?" Raj yelled at Robert.

"Far away from here," Robert yelled back without turning his head. "It's about time someone buried the ghost once and for all."

"Wait!" cried Raj.

He stumbled to his feet and ran to catch up with Robert. Robert didn't bother to turn around, but Raj caught up and walked beside him.

"I'm sorry," Raj blurted out. "I'm sorry for everything."

Robert smirked at him through his pain.

"Apology accepted," he replied. "Now go home. We've both had a long past couple of days."

"No," said Raj plainly. "I won't go home until you answer another question."

Robert looked at him and sighed.

"All right kid. Make it quick."

Raj nodded and cleared his throat before continuing.

"If I'm on the hit list, then that means you must have some information on me. Who am I, and where did I come from?"

Robert shrugged.

"I don't know," he replied. "I tried my best to get it out of her, but she wouldn't tell me anything."

Raj walked in silence for a moment. It seemed he would never get answers to who he was, and why he was there. But there was one more question which burned in his mind.

"Why didn't you kill me?" he asked. "Not even just right now. I mean from the first time we met."

Robert limped along, holding his tongue as if he had nothing to say. But Raj saw the look in his eyes, and could tell the memories were all coming back to him.

"Because you remind me of an old friend," he admitted. "When I looked at you the first time, I saw him looking back at me. I couldn't bear to watch him die again."

Tears welled in Raj's eyes. He heard the pain in Robert's voice, and felt it in every word he spoke. That someone was Robert's best friend. And even though Raj could never know this person, his resemblance to him made

Robert's life a little happier. It all made sense now. Why Robert had spared him the first night they met. Why he'd saved him from the junkyard and nursed him back to health. Raj wanted to ask more, but Robert stopped walking and turned towards him.

"You gotta turn around now, kid. If I won't kill you, crossing that line surely will."

"No, wait!" cried Raj. "I don't have a zone tag, so I can go with you. See?"

Raj pulled up his sleeve and showed Robert the underside of his forearm. Raj's arm didn't bear the telltale injection scar, but a very distinct glisten caught Robert's eye. He grabbed Raj's arm and studied it closely. Raj began to question him, but Robert shushed him. On the upper part of the forearm, Robert saw the slight glimmer of the ultraviolet insignia tattooed into his skin.

"Project Blue Steel," he whispered.

More memories of the past flooded into his mind, but Robert fought not to dwell on them.

"C'mon!" he shouted as he took off towards his motorcycle.

Raj hurried along as Robert ripped the motorcycle off the ground and brought the engine to life.

"Get on!" Robert yelled.

Raj wasn't sure what to make of the whole ordeal. One moment Robert was telling him to turn around, the next he was asking him to tag along for the ride.

"Where are we going?" he asked.

Robert looked at him with a fire in his eyes.

"To get your answers."

Chapter 20: A Spark in the Kindling

"Everything is so......bright."

Raj struggled to keep up with Robert as he led him away from the alley where they hid the motorcycle. Even so, he couldn't help but grin from ear to ear. His feet pattered along the spotless streets as he gazed past the blinding streetlamps at the pristine buildings towering overhead. It wasn't what Raj had imagined, but he'd finally made it to Zone 2.

But even with all the excitement, Raj couldn't help but notice Robert's stunning pace. There was no way anyone should be walking after being clotheslined by a steel cable. Yet Robert's limp had disappeared as if the incident had never happened.

"What are you?" asked Raj.

Robert kept his head forward and continued walking.

"The same thing you are," he replied. "We are both property of the government, created by a secret experimental division that dates back well before either of us was born."

Raj had so many questions, but kept quiet to let Robert continue his explanation.

"Project Blue Steel began in the early 1950's for the sole purpose of modifying man to overcome his own physical limitations. Whether the modification is genetic or physical, we are all created with a specific purpose in mind."

"And what is that?" asked Raj.

"War," Robert replied bluntly. "Different terrains, climates, and enemies. We are designed to be the apex predator of our specific ecosystem. Though the project also worked on modifications for purposes like longer life and disease resistance."

Raj took a moment to digest Robert's words.

"So what does that make me?" he asked. "What does that make *you*?"

Robert reached into his inner breast pocket and found two crinkled cigarettes he just remembered were there. He then placed one in his mouth and lit the end into a cinder.

"I am one of the earliest accidental successes at making the perfect soldier," he said as he exhaled the smoke in his lungs.

Robert took another drag before continuing.

"My father was a very smart man. He was the head of quite a few projects run by the government, and is responsible for creating the serum which made me the way I am. My mother died minutes after giving birth to me. I was born premature with a rare degenerative disease. It left my father with a tough choice, but a perfect opportunity. He had been working on what he called 'The Miracle Genes.' This specific serum was designed to make cells over one thousand times more resilient for a life outside Earth. And since he used his own DNA for the experiment, there were only two people it would work on— me, and him. Three days after the injection I was healthier and stronger than any newborn the doctor had ever seen."

"That's incredible!" exclaimed Raj.

"It is," replied Robert, "but my father and the other project leaders soon found out that wasn't the end of its capabilities. My body heals and grows incredibly fast. Broken bones heal within days, not weeks. Deep gashes will completely close within hours, looking like there was never a scratch. My strength is triple what one would expect from a man my size, and my body remains youthful for substantially longer than a normal human being. My father didn't know it, but he successfully created the world's first super soldier."

"Wow," said Raj. "Who is your father? He must be famous."

Robert shrugged.

"He is. But no one knows him for that bit of work. Just....everything else he's done. Like this."

Robert pointed a finger up to the sky, and Raj's gaze followed it upward. He looked up in awe, almost falling backwards in an attempt to see the top of the seemingly limitless building.

"Phoenix Tower," Raj murmured.

He'd dreamed of this day ever since he could remember, but his dreams were not enough to prepare him for it. The crystal-clear faces showed a perfect reflection of the surrounding cityscape, and the colored accents rose high up the building's flanks. It was absolutely perfect.

"Sebastian Phoenix is your father," Raj said with astonishment.

Robert continued to look towards the top and simply nodded. The pieces continued to fit together in Raj's head.

"But that would make you..."

"Old enough to be your great grandfather, yea," finished Robert. "I lost count at fifty-five."

Robert took one last pull of his cigarette and flicked it down the street.

"But enough about me, kid," exhaled Robert. "Any answers you seek, we will find them in there."

Robert and Raj continued the short stroll to the main entrance of the tower. They reached it, and Raj wrenched heavily on the door. It did not move an inch, remaining firmly within its frame.

"How are we going to get in there?" asked Raj.

Robert reached into his bag and opened up his copy of *The Gatekeeper's Key*. He pulled out a plastic bag containing the chip Joe had given him and swiped the chip at the sensor.

"Access granted," chimed the door as it slid open. "Welcome, Leonard Smeebly."

Robert stowed the chip and casually walked through the passageway with Raj in tow. The lobby was dark except for the single light shining down upon the stone phoenix in the middle of the room.

"Wow," whispered Raj.

He found himself awestruck by the beauty, and would have stared at it all night if Robert had not pulled him towards the elevators. Raj's face lit up again as he looked forward to see the doors of the elevator glide open. Robert rolled his eyes and dragged Raj in with him. He had to slap Raj's hand a couple times to stop him from pressing all the buttons, but finally swiped his faux clearance for the top level. The doors then closed before the elevator sped up the shaft.

"So how did you get, you know, out *there*?" Raj asked.

Robert looked at the elevator doors as if looking into the past.

"The short story is that I was a wanted criminal. Before that, I served the old government during the resource war, and acted as a main player in the coup which brought the new regime into power. In the final days of the war, my sister sent my squad on what turned out to be a suicide mission. I went against my orders and made a call that saved my squad that day, and led to my squad saving countless other lives. Despite the outcome, my superiors set out to put me on trial and send me to Eisenstadt. When I was in jail waiting for my court date, I realized that I had been fighting for the majority of my life. I was tired of it. I still am. All I wanted was peace and quiet. So, with a little bit of innovation, and a few strokes of luck, I made my way out of the HIVE and went on the run."

"But why would they do that?" Raj asked. "Why would they condemn you for saving people?"

"I wasn't quite sure back then," replied Robert. "But coming back after decades of being gone, I think my sister wanted to get rid of me. Before that mission, I found out my sister had plans to selectively breed the population of New Amsterdam to make a populace predisposed to obedience and brainwashing. Because I had an equal share in the company, I also had a say in the decision. Naturally, I said no."

"You think your own sister would get rid of you just for that?"

"Well, I wouldn't put it past her. The HIVE used to be different before I left. Don't get me wrong, there was still inequality between the zones, but not like this. From what I've seen, that's exactly what she's done."

Raj thought it over for a moment.

"But why would she bother to selectively breed in the first place?" he asked. "It doesn't make sense."

Robert sighed and shook his head

"You really don't get it, kid? The people in Zone 2 won't ask much past what they're told. When something happens, all the government has to do is put together a plausible story and let the media take care of the rest. Those who don't fit the criteria get thrown in zones where the only rule is do what you need to survive. As far as the HIVE is concerned, anything is legal in the lower zones. People that need to put all of their energy towards survival rarely have any energy left to fight the system oppressing them."

Raj let the information steep in his head for a moment before replying.

"So why not kill us? I mean, I'm glad to be alive, but why keep us around?"

"As a workforce, and as a pool to recruit leaders," Robert replied. "The trade-off for breeding for more compliance is the loss of intelligence and free thought, and both are qualities needed to run businesses, lead armies, or govern cities."

The elevator doors slid open, and Robert led Raj down the quick hallway to the main part of the suite. Raj was ready to stroll right in, but Robert put an arm out and stopped him.

"There might be someone in there," he whispered.

Robert pulled out his gun and walked through the double doors. Although everything looked quiet, Robert still crept around the room to thoroughly check all the corners. Once he was satisfied he waved for Raj to enter.

"No one's here. We're all clear."

Robert walked over to Marcella's desk and turned on her computer while Raj wandered around the suite. The sheer elegance and neatness of the room left him dumbfounded. Robert rolled his eyes again, but knew he couldn't blame him. Someone who spent his whole life in the lower zones couldn't possibly imagine anything being this nice in real life.

The computer finally loaded up to the home screen before prompting a clearance code from Robert. He looked down at his wrist top and began typing away.

"Ok girl, it's time for you to work your magic," he said to his wrist top.

By this time Raj was at the bar examining the endless array of bottles behind the counter.

"What is this stuff?" he asked, picking up a bottle.

"Alcohol," said Robert shortly. "Trust me, it's an acquired taste."

Raj popped the cork out and took a whiff. The strong smell of whiskey filled his nostrils, causing him to jolt his head back and recork the bottle.

"You're probably right," he said, holding back his urge to puke as he replaced the bottle back on the shelf.

Robert continued to watch the screen as he plugged away on his wrist top. After a few more seconds of scrolling code, the computer signed in as Marcella and granted him full access.

"Haha, BINGO!"

He engaged the uplink between his wrist top and the computer and immediately began downloading all files. Robert read the expected completion time of twenty minutes and grimaced.

"Twenty minutes more than I would like, but it's worth the risk. There's definitely something I can use as leverage."

With the download in progress, Robert turned his attention to manually finding the files.

"Let's see now...." he said to himself.

He scanned through the folders on the computer looking for any classified files. It wasn't long before one in particular caught his eye.

"Operation Phoenix Rising," he murmured.

Robert's mind traveled back to the night Aesculus visited him on mission. His target had mentioned Operation Phoenix Rising before he died, but he hadn't given any solid information. Without even thinking about it, Robert opened the folder. Inside, he found the unedited files of all his targets and began reading them aloud.

"Samantha Irving, Chief Criminal Investigator.......George Penn, VP of NytCorp; Phoenix Technologies' top competitor......Anthony Greene, Financial Director, Phoenix Technologies."

Robert's suspicions were confirmed with each consecutive file he read. This was a list of anyone who threatened her reign, and Robert was the hand with which she struck them down. But even in this lengthy list, Raj's file was nowhere to be found. Robert clicked on a subfolder to see if it was misplaced, but instead found an operations log filled with entries. Chills ran down his spine as he saw the last entry was written a little over an hour ago.

September 4, 2085 10:34 PM

Robert has done well with his list; almost better than expected. Yet, he still hasn't led us to the location of the core. At this point most would assume that the intel is false, but I'm not convinced. My father loved to speak in riddles, but one thing he never did was lie. Robert might not be willing to give up his secrets, but we'll get them out of him.

I sent him on one more mission to take care of another liability like him. Dr. Raj will not be happy, but he should feel lucky I don't dispose of him too for letting the subject go. We are on the cusp of creating the genetic modification to disrupt the link between intelligence and free thought, and I still need him to complete that.

Once Robert completes his final task, he will be captured and sent to Eisenstadt. He is a liability. The only place he won't interfere with our plans is a dark cell deep within the depths of hell. I give him three weeks until he goes mad and tells us everything. Once he does, we will unlock the secrets of free energy and be able to begin Operation Firestorm.

Marcella

"That fucking bitch!" yelled Robert.

"What happened?" asked Raj. "What did you find?"

Robert stood up and slammed his fists on the desk, sending cracks throughout its glass face.

"You fucked up, Marcella!" he shouted. "You're gonna pay!"

Raj walked over to the desk and saw a rage in Robert's eyes he had never seen before. But before Raj could calm him down, the ding of the elevator drew their attention towards the hall. Without hesitation, Robert drew his pistol and emptied his entire clip into the doors.

"Floor One Hundred and Twenty-Three: Phoenix Suite."

Robert reloaded as the doors slid open, but he soon realized there was no need. The armed guards lying in the elevator were no longer a threat.

"Uhh, Robert," said Raj as he tapped Robert on the shoulder. "Look down there."

Robert turned around and looked down at the group of security robots gathering on the lawn.

Robert sighed and shook his head.

"Looks like we've got company."

CHAPTER 21: THE FLAMES IGNITE

A silence lingered in the air as Raj watched Robert counting the forces below, but the ding of the elevator sliding closed brought Robert's attention back to the room. He ran over to the hallway to see the numbers above the elevator working their way towards zero.

Raj looked out the window by the bar and anxiously peered back towards Robert. "What do we do?" he asked. "They keep coming from everywhere!"

Robert turned to Raj and tossed him his pistol.

"Here, take this," he ordered.

Raj fumbled it, but managed to grab it before it fell to the ground.

"You have dual-wielded pistols before, right?" asked Robert. "I mean, they had to have gone over weapons training with you."

Raj shook his head.

"Gun training was next week."

Robert laughed to himself at the irony of the situation and began to walk over to Raj.

"Now it makes sense why you left the safety on before. Here, you just—"

The sound of gunfire emanating from the hallway stopped Robert mid-sentence. The bullets ripped through Robert's arm and torso as he stumbled and fell away from the entrance.

"GET DOWN!" he yelled as he rolled onto the floor and pulled out the sub-machine gun slung tightly under his coat.

Within an instant guards poured into the room with guns drawn. Robert stemmed the flow with his sub-machine gun, but Raj jumped over the bar and took cover.

"What do I do?" he cried.

"Mine is loaded!" bellowed Robert between bursts. "Point and shoot!"

Raj's whole body trembled as he attempted to poke his head above the bar. Stray shots shattered the bottles behind him and ripped through the bar, freezing him in place. But the gunfire momentarily stopped, and Raj mustered up enough courage to poke his head up. At least half a dozen men lay silent on the floor as Robert used one arm to drag himself towards the bar.

"Cover me, kid!" he yelled as he reloaded.

But just as he said that, two more men breached the entrance and turned towards their position. Raj froze with fear. He knew he had to shoot, but his body wouldn't let him. Robert must have sensed this because he let out a deafening roar.

"RAAAJ!!!"

Raj closed his eyes and pulled the trigger. The gun jumped to life, nearly throwing itself from his hand. Raj almost let go, but he held a firm grip and continued to pull the trigger until the whole room once again fell silent. Raj opened his eyes to the sight of fallen men piled at the doorway. He vaulted back over the bar, only to be greeted by a gruesome scene. Bullet wounds riddled Robert's body, visible through the holes in his clothes. But to Raj's surprise, Robert wasn't dead. His body had already stemmed the bleeding and started the process of its recovery.

"Knew I could count on you, kid," said Robert as he motioned for Raj to help him up. "Not as young as I used to be. That would have been a piece of cake in my sixties."

Raj helped Robert to his feet and brushed the dust off his coat.

"So if you can age, can you die too?" he asked.

"I hope so, kid," replied Robert as he winced and clutched his side. "We all gotta die someday, and I'd rather it be my body than my soul."

Those simple words left Raj speechless. Anyone would certainly kill for immortality. Yet here was Robert with the possibility of living forever, and he was hoping for an end. But before Raj could explore the thought more, the sight of Robert limping towards the hallway brought him back to the reality of the situation.

"It's clear for now," Robert said over his shoulder. "What's the progress on the download?"

Raj darted to the desk and checked the screen.

"Sixty-two percent," he confirmed.

"It's not going fast enough," Robert said to himself.

He poked his head down the hallway and assessed the situation. The numbers above the elevator climbed as the sound of clicking boots echoed from the stairwell.

"Get ready, kid!" Robert yelled. "We're going to have some company soon."

The steps grew louder and louder until they stopped altogether. Robert peeked into the hallway just in time for the ding of the elevator doors sliding open to break the silence. Robert kept his gun aimed, but soon realized there was no one inside. Instead he found himself staring down the barrel of an anti-personnel robot.

"GET DOWN!" Robert yelled as he dove for cover.

A hollow thud emanated from the hallway, and Robert shielded his eyes just in time to protect them from the blinding light of the flash-bang grenade. White noise filled his ears, and he opened his eyes to see a red light pulsing through the suite. By a stroke of luck, the force of the blast had blown out an already damaged window and set off the emergency lockdown. Robert let out a sigh of relief as a solid metal door came down from the ceiling to block the entrance.

The pounding of fists on the door grew louder as Robert regained his hearing, but so did a groaning from across the room. Robert looked over to find Raj underneath the desk writhing in pain.

"You're ok, kid," called Robert as he pushed himself off the ground and closed in on Raj. "I remember my first flash-bang. You'll be good in a minute."

He pulled Raj from under the desk and held him for a moment to make sure he could stand on his own.

"Flash-bang set off the security door," Robert pointed out.

"So we're trapped in here?" Raj asked anxiously.

"Relax, kid," Robert assured him, "we've got this."

In reality, Robert wasn't sure of his next move. Jumping out the broken window would be extremely risky. His glide wings were only meant to hold one. He could give them to Raj, but that would leave Robert with only two options: fight, or jump. He checked his pockets to find he only had three magazines worth of ammo left. Tackling them head-on would be suicide, but a fall from such a height would have the same effect.

The pounding on the door continued as Robert tried to think. The anxiety and doubt leaked from the cracks of his mind, but he knew he had to calm it. He turned around to lean on the desk, closed his eyes, and took a few deep breaths. The surrounding sounds died out one by one until all he heard was his own heartbeat. Robert then opened his eyes and saw his reflection in the window.

Months had passed since he last looked at himself in the mirror at the Phoenix Estate, but gazing into his own eyes brought him back to that very moment. If he'd known then what would happen, he never would have walked through the bookcase. But just as he thought that, the words from his father's letter ran through his head.

"Whenever you feel weak, the mirror can show you strength you never knew existed."

Robert looked into the reflection of the window and saw the same bookcase sitting on the wall past the bar. Suddenly everything made sense. He turned around as the noise of his surroundings flooded back into his head. The banging and screaming on the other side of the door mixed with Raj's panic as he paced the room.

"We're trapped in here, Robert!" he cried. "We can't possibly fight them all! Snap out of it, Robert!"

"No, you snap out of it!" Robert warned. "Prey animals panic right before they become a meal. Do not panic. We are going to get out of here."

Raj calmed down a bit as Robert riffled through his bag.

"We have about ten minutes before they get through that door," continued Robert. "That should be more than we need."

Robert pulled out the copy of *The Gatekeeper's Key* and strode over to the bookcase. He studied the books and looked for a pattern.

"This isn't the time to be checking out some light reading," complained Raj.

Robert ignored him, too transfixed on the task at hand to listen to his concerns. After a minute of looking, he finally noticed a pattern among the aged books lining the shelf. All the books on the middle row were written by Charles Sunterberry— the author of *The Gatekeeper's Key*. Oddly enough, there was already a copy of it on the shelf. Robert pulled it out of its snug spot to find the book much lighter than his own copy.

"Enough of this!" cried Raj, too anxious to sit around any longer.

He snatched Robert's copy of the book from his hand and slammed it back into the bookshelf.

"We don't have time for this! If you haven't noticed, we're tra—"

Raj stopped mid-sentence as the entire wall around the bookcase grew a pearlescent sheen before disappearing altogether. The lights behind the bookcase flickered on to reveal a secret room. Robert handed the other copy of the book to a baffled Raj and strode past the bookcase. The book slipped from Raj's hands and crashed to the floor with a thud. The pages flew open, forcing a metallic object from its folds. Raj looked down to see a large, gold-plated key resting on the floor next to the hollowed pages of the book.

"The key," Raj murmured to himself as he picked it up off the floor.

He examined the house and inscription etched into opposite sides of the key's handle. Raj thought finding the key could be a coincidence, but the tingling feeling down his spine told him otherwise. The voice in the dream had told him to find it. But who was that voice, and why did he need Raj? But now was not the time to ask, so Raj pocketed the key and went after Robert into the secret room.

Research equipment dotted almost the entire room, but what caught Raj's eye was a mannequin next to a large wooden desk towards the back of the room. Raj made his way over to it and inspected the sleek vest it was wearing.

"This thing looks useful," said Raj as he removed the vest. "Might be bulletproof."

Robert was nearby, checking out the emergency escape elevator hidden behind some junk. It had a gate like an old service elevator, but was only large enough to fit a single person. Robert turned around to break the news, but stopped when he saw Raj slipping on the vest.

"Wait, No!" Robert shouted, but it was too late.

Raj zipped up the front of the vest and instantly felt the needle-like projections pierce the length of his spine. A new energy ran through his body as Raj saw the projection of a Head's Up Display loading in the air in front of him. He fell to his knees as the energy intensified. His muscles weren't responding to him; even his voice failed him. Just when the energy became unbearable, it stopped.

"Synchronization complete," said the vest. "Welcome. I am a third-generation Combat and Bionic Assistance Device developed by Phoenix Technologies. But you can call me Kate."

"Incredible," Robert said to himself.

He walked over to Raj and examined the vest while he helped him back to his feet. The seamless vest held a small backpack-like pouch on the back, as well as small pouches on the front. A thin metal frame like the one which attached Robert's gauntlets to his nervous system poked out by the neck. It was obviously made by his father, but it was still a prototype Robert wasn't familiar with.

"What are your capabilities, Kate?" Robert asked.

"The primary capabilities of the current Model S attachment include danger assessment and mitigation, stealth cloaking, and strength enhancement," she replied. "Upon special request, Advanced Survival Assistance is also equipped."

Robert patted Raj on the back and led him towards the emergency elevator.

"Good find, kid," he said. "Now we gotta get you outta here."

But as Robert turned around, his eyes landed on something he'd only seen once before. Resting within a glass showcase in front of the desk was a clear cube with a fiery ball floating inside. Robert slipped past Raj but froze as he saw his name written on a folded piece of paper next to the cube. He didn't believe it, but the unmistakable handwriting left him without a doubt. Robert opened the case and grabbed the paper before unfolding it and reading its contents.

My Dearest Robert,

I'm writing this to you because I am certain you will be the person smart enough to find it first. Inside this workshop you will find top-secret technology powered by the same power source sitting next to this letter. I'm sorry I didn't tell you earlier, but secrecy has been my top priority. This strange looking cube is only one of the two Phoenix Cores used to build this very building.

I could drown you with the details, but unfortunately my time is running short. You need to keep this tech safe, including the core powering the entire city. Open that door for no one. There are too many who would abuse the power of a sun, but I know you are not one of them.

Trust yourself and keep strong.

Sebastian Phoenix.

P.S. - Activating the Phoenix Core when it's not under load will lead to.... explosive consequences. Even you aren't that bulletproof.

Robert read the letter over and over, digesting every word. The cube he used as a flashlight wasn't just an example of Phoenix Technologies' capabilities, it was the most advanced technology Phoenix Technologies had ever made. How did he not know he held the power to take over the world? Maybe his father was right. Robert never knew because he never sought to abuse the power.

But before Robert could think about it more, Raj shook him back into reality.

"You ok?" he asked. "We need to go!"

The banging on the door grew into a loud and rhythmic thud, telling Robert their time was running short. He led Raj to the emergency elevator and pulled open the gate before pushing him inside.

"You aren't safe in the HIVE," said Robert as he closed the gate. "Go straight down the road we walked to get here and go through the processing station at the end of that road. The departure terminal will take you to the unguarded side of the bridge. If I'm not there by sunrise, move on."

"Wait, I can't leave The Order!" protested Raj. "And I can't leave you to die up here and leave me stranded out there!"

"You have no choice, kid," replied Robert. "You have a target on your back here. Besides, you have Advanced Survival Assistance now. They used to give the grunts Basic Survival Assistance back in the war. If they can survive with that, you'll be fine."

Robert pushed a button on the outside wall and watched Raj descend the shaft.

"See you on the other side!" he yelled before heading back towards the suite.

Robert thought about grabbing as much tech as possible, but knew Marcella could never get to it without the book. He walked out of the workshop and pulled his copy of *The Gatekeeper's Key* from the shelf. The wall reappeared within an instant, hiding the secrets of the room from unwanted eyes. He then walked behind the bar, grabbed a few bottles, and went over to the computer to find the download completed. Robert untethered his wrist top from the computer and stepped over to the blown-out window. As he looked down on the city below, the relentless pounding behind him stopped. Quiet fell upon the suite until an all-too-familiar voice cut the silence.

"Robert, I know it's you in there," it shouted through the steel door.

Robert stepped back from the ledge and turned back towards the door.

"Marcella, is that you?" he shouted.

"Yes, Robert. Now open the door so we can get this whole fiasco settled."

Robert looked towards the bookcase and thought about his father's words. It was his job to keep the core safe. The smart way to do that meant gliding out the window and meeting Raj on the outside, but the fire burning inside him could not be ignored. He pulled a cloth-covered object from his bag and unwrapped it to let its glow light his face. Robert stared into the fiery depths of his Phoenix Core and cracked a smile.

"Sure, Marcella. Let's talk."

CHAPTER 22: THE THIRD STEP

The emergency elevator clunked to a stop at the end of a dark, musty tunnel. Raj stepped out and closed the gate behind him before sending the elevator back up the shaft. The dim lights dotting the path before him stretched indefinitely down the tunnel. Instead of seeing near darkness, Kate enhanced Raj's vision enough for him to pinpoint the escape ladder almost one thousand feet away. Her amazing capabilities allowed Raj to continue forward without concern.

His shoes slapped against the damp floor, occasionally splashing in the shallow puddles accumulating in the low spots. The surreal calmness was a stark contrast to what Raj imagined was happening above him. But as Raj thought back to the chaos atop Phoenix Tower, he thought about his friends back in the lower zones. He didn't want to leave them, but he also realized how hard it would be to face them after letting Rook's killer go free. Raj wanted to blame Marcella, but he knew it had been Robert's choice to pull the trigger. The dilemma played out in his head until he reached the ladder at the end of the tunnel.

The crude steel ladder stretched up about twenty feet to a sewer cap at street level. Raj ascended the ladder and lifted the cap to find himself in an alley on the opposite side of the lawn. The security robots maintained rank on the lawn as if waiting for Robert to step out the front door.

"Robert," he said into his wrist top as he climbed all the way out of the tunnel, "I'm at ground level. Where are you?"

Silence filled the radio waves as Raj attempted to contact him again. But before he could, Kate's voice broke the silence.

"Energy anomaly detected."

"What?" whispered Raj. "What do you mean by that?"

Before Kate could reply, a loud crash emanated from atop the tower. Raj's gaze darted upward just in time to see a ball of light zoom skyward through the roof. The light grew with intensity before changing direction and bolting back down towards the tower. It crashed through the roof with increasing speed, penetrating about fifty floors before erupting into a blinding light. Raj shielded his eyes and braced himself for the inevitable shock-wave. The glass-shattering wave ripped past him, followed by the deafening roar of the explosion. Debris shot past him at lightning speed, but somehow Raj held his ground. When it stopped, he uncovered his eyes to find a twisted stub where the tower once stood.

"Robert!" he yelled.

Despite Raj's call, Robert was nowhere to be seen. However, some of the robots heard his scream and started in his direction.

"Hostiles approaching," said Kate.

Raj stood there in disbelief. He expected to see Robert come swooping down from the cloud of dust forming above his head, or to wake up back in his bed.

"This can't be real," he said to himself. "Robert always makes it. He'll get out of this alive."

"Hostiles approaching," repeated Kate. "We are outnumbered. The best course of action would be to flee."

Still, Raj remained planted to the floor in a daze.

"Let's go!" yelled Kate.

Raj's body sprang into life and sprinted down the street without his consent. He gained control after a moment, but at the same time felt the almost instinctual urge pushing his body to keep going. Even with this extra boost, the security bots weren't far behind. They closed in fast on his tail and were soon within striking distance. Their fruitless attempts at commanding Raj to stop were followed by a barrage of lightning bolts aimed in his direction. Raj's body zig-zagged without his consent, dodging each shot as if he had eyes in the back of his head.

"More hostiles are closing in," warned Kate. "We can't keep this up for much longer."

Raj's body veered harder and faster as the lightning bolts whizzing past his head doubled in number. His legs and lungs burned with pain, and he could feel his footing almost give out with each change of direction. He closed his eyes and let the unknown force take control until a loud crash caused him to look back. By a stroke of luck, a piece of debris the size of a bus landed in the street behind him. It crushed the security bots as it tumbled between the buildings and closed in on Raj. His guiding force veered down a side street, steering Raj out of the debris' path. The force turned him back onto a street heading in his original direction, and continued to push forward.

"We need to get out of here before any more hostiles show up," said Kate. "Where are we going?"

"To the motorcycle!" yelled Raj in between breaths.

"Yes, but where after that?" she asked.

"Home!" shouted Raj.

Another piece of debris came crashing down mere feet behind him, and the shock-wave caused him to lose his footing. He flew forward and watched the ground inch closer to his face before everything went black.

#

Chirping. Rustling. Foreign noises he'd never heard before. A cool breeze tickled his wet face, but it was also overcome with a warming sensation he could almost see through his eyelids. The air smelled different, yet comforting and familiar. Raj's eyes slowly opened to take in the world around him. He was on his back, staring into a vibrant blue sky dotted with fluffy white masses.

"What are those?" Raj said to himself.

"Clouds," replied Kate. "Have you never seen one?"

Raj watched the clouds change shape above him as they floated on their way. He lost himself in their acrobatic dance across the sky, but the twirling clouds brought back his last waking memories. The tower... Robert... Raj needed to find him and report back to The Order. He tried to push himself off the ground, but was only met with pain. It shot through his bad shoulder, causing him to drop back to the floor.

"Take it easy," said Kate. "Your body has been through a lot."

Raj readjusted his position and felt the strange ground under his tired legs. He saw the tall grass surrounding him and wondered how he'd ended up at the Tree of Hope.

"Where's Robert? Am I... dead?" he asked.

"My survival protocol kicked in, and I decided our best chance for survival was fleeing to our point of interest," replied Kate. "Your body suffered some injuries, including a torn rotator cuff and a dislocated shoulder. Both on the same side. I relocated the shoulder and injected regeneration gel into your system to repair the tear. The vehicle operation protocol included in the survival database allowed me to operate Robert's motorcycle and get us home. So no, you are not dead."

"Wait," said Raj, "you can do that? Just take over my body?"

"Yes, and no," she replied. "Think of me as a second brain. If my survival protocol kicks in, I can steer you away from danger. In the event you are unconscious and in danger, I can take full control to ensure your survival."

Raj lay there and thought about it for a minute.

"So you're pretty much a part of me."

"Correct," she responded. "Once my brain becomes calibrated with yours, we will operate as one. Your survival is my survival."

"Well, that's good to know," added Raj.

"As for Robert," she continued, "there were no readable signs of life in our general area during or after the explosion."

Raj let those words sink in as the pain trickled from his core. First Rook, now Robert. Candice was all he had left, and he couldn't bear to lose her too. The thought of Candice put a fire in his heart, and he used his good arm to push his upper body off the ground. The tall grass continued to block his vision of his surroundings, but Raj noticed Robert's motorcycle parked a few feet away.

"Where are we?" he asked.

"We are home."

Raj spun his body around to get a better look. This was not home, nor was it the Tree of Hope. The grass was way too tall.

"This is not home," he said.

"Negative," Kate disagreed. "This is the preset destination for home."

Raj mustered enough strength to lift himself off the ground and gasped as his vision broke above the grass. The decrepit buildings he expected to see at the edge of the field were replaced by trees full of luscious green leaves. The rays of sunlight shining through the canopy warmed his face as the grass surrounding him rustled in a calm breeze.

"This is beautiful," he whispered. "You sure I'm not dead?"

"Yes, I'm sure," assured Kate. "Your survival is my survival, remember?"

Raj stood silent for a moment and took it all in.

"So we're...."

"Not in the HIVE anymore, no."

Raj couldn't talk, as he was too overwhelmed by the beauty of the outside world. But even the beauty couldn't keep the sinking feeling in his stomach at bay. His home, family, and way of life lay trapped behind the walls of a city out to get him, and the only person able to guide him through this strange new world had disappeared within the explosion that engulfed Phoenix Tower.

The fear bubbling within turned into chills as Raj turned around and gazed upon the mossy building behind him. He pulled the key from his pocket and once again examined the building etched into the handle.

"This can't be," he said to himself.

The building on the key was a perfect match to the one standing a few hundred feet away. Raj flipped over the key and looked at the inscription on the other side.

"Kate, what does this say?" he asked.

"The inscription is Latin for 'Embrace The Unknown.'"

Raj could no longer doubt the key's significance after hearing those words. He didn't know what was waiting for him inside, but the words etched into the key gave him the courage to move forward. Raj walked the worn path to the building and up the old stone steps. He met the iron door atop the stairs and ripped away at the mossy patches until he found the oblong keyhole above the basin. Raj raised the key to the hole, his shaky hand missing it a few times before it finally slid into place.

But instead of turning the key, he froze. The force driving him forward moments earlier stopped him in his tracks, making him second guess his next move. Raj looked back upon the field and out towards the trees. The feeling in his stomach told him this was his last chance to turn back. He could walk away right now and have Kate take him home, or he could face the mystery on the other side of the door. The wind rippling towards him through the grass climbed the steps and caressed his face, and at that moment Raj found his answer. He thought about Candice one last time before turning around and spinning the key.

A sting in his hand caused him to pull back, and he noticed the blood-soaked pin now protruding from the bow of the key. A single drop of blood fell into the basin, bringing the inner mechanisms of the door to life. They clunked and turned until the door freed itself from the wall.

"Welcome, Lieutenant Bernard," greeted an automated voice.

"So that's who he is," said Raj as he walked through the entrance.

The lights flickered on as he entered, illuminating the dusty room. But before he ventured any farther, a familiar voice called to him from his right.

"Over here."

Raj looked over to the door to his right and approached with care. He pushed the door open to find a cluttered study. A large portrait hung above the paper-strewn desk in front of him, and an opening next to the bookcase on his right led into another room. The voice called out once again from the plush, backwards-facing swivel chair behind the desk.

"It seems you have made it. I'm proud of you, but it's not time for you to rest. Your journey has just begun."

At that moment, Raj recognized the voice as the one from his dreams.

"All right, Lieutenant Bernard," Raj called back. "It's time for you to explain what's going on."

"Oh, I'm not Lieutenant Bernard," replied the voice.

The chair turned around to reveal a hologram of an older, gray-haired man.

"I am Sebastian Phoenix."

EPILOGUE

The moonlight reflecting off the swimming pool in the back yard shined through the window of the dark room. A fire crackling on the far side of the large study illuminated the room just enough to outline the figure resting in silence behind the desk. A loud knock on the door rang through the room, interrupting the silence.

"Come in," called the figure.

Commander Aesculus walked in through the door and approached the desk.

"I'm here for the status report," he said in a deep voice.

He was met with silence, so he continued.

"The tower is completely destroyed, along with the atmospheric field generator and transmitter. The wall is the only thing keeping us from full exposure to the elements."

Aesculus waited for a reply, but he was greeted with more silence.

"Initial reports also show the zone barriers are temporarily down, but we do have a cover story already submitted to the press for release in the morning news."

Still silence.

"However, there is some good news."

Aesculus reached into his inside pocket and pulled out a glowing cube which illuminated the immediate area.

"We managed to recover this. Not sure what it is yet, but we believe it to be a Phoenix Core."

He held it out above the desk, illuminating the feminine figure sitting in the chair.

"What do you think, Senator Phoenix?" Aesculus asked.

Marcella grabbed the cube and brought it up to her face. The soft glow showed the small smile she cracked through her thin lips.

"This is excellent, Commander," she said. "Despite a few hiccups, our plan is running smoothly."

She handed the cube back to Aesculus, who stuffed it back into his pocket.

"Commence with Operation Firestorm," she continued.

Aesculus nodded his head and turned to leave the room. Marcella rose from her chair and looked out the window into the back yard. She smiled as the moonlight shined upon her face.

"Yes," she whispered. "Everything seems to be falling into place."

ABOUT THE AUTHOR

Brendan Landry is a self-published author from New York. Born and raised in the Hudson Valley, he graduated from Ramapo College in New Jersey with a degree in Environmental Science. He is an avid photographer, and loves to spend his spare time hiking, cruising the backroads on his motorcycle, and playing his guitar and banjo. If you would like to know more about Brendan, or stay updated on his future publications, be sure to visit his website www.brendanlandry.com